"Don't Go, Kelly."

Beau leaned forward to kiss her. "Last time I was your indulgence, so how about indulging me this time?"

She saw the lingering pain in his eyes. "You're not an indulgence, Beau. You weren't then, and you're not now. I was nervous, and I said some things I didn't mean. Please believe me."

He smiled. "When you look at me like that, I'd believe night were day." He regarded her with unnerving intensity. "You know, I think you take responsibility not only for things that aren't your fault but for things that haven't happened yet."

"What do you mean?"

"You worry about what people will think about us being lovers before we're even there yet. One night does not lovers make."

"Oh, no?"

"No," he assured her in a teasing voice. "Usually it takes at least two."

Dear Reader:

Welcome! You hold in your hand a Silhouette Desire—your ticket to a whole new world of reading pleasure.

A Silhouette Desire is a sensuous, contemporary romance about passions, problems and the ultimate power of love. It is about today's woman—intelligent, successful, giving—but it is also the story of a romance between two people who are strong enough to follow their own individual paths, yet strong enough to compromise, as well.

These books are written by, for and about every woman that you are—wife, mother, sister, lover, daughter, career woman. A Silhouette Desire heroine must face the same challenges, achieve the same successes, in her story as you do in your own life.

The Silhouette reader is not afraid to enjoy herself. She knows when to take things seriously and when to indulge in a fantasy world. With six books a month, Silhouette Desire strives to meet her many moods, but each book is always a compelling love story.

Make a commitment to romance—go wild with Silhouette Desire!

Best,

Isabel Swift
Senior Editor & Editorial Coordinator

ELAINE CAMP
The Second Mr. Sullivan

Published by Silhouette Books New York

America's Publisher of Contemporary Romance

SILHOUETTE BOOKS
300 East 42nd St., New York, N.Y. 10017

Copyright © 1988 by Deborah E. Camp

All rights reserved, including the right to reproduce
this book or portions thereof in any form whatsoever.
For information address Silhouette Books,
300 East 42nd St., New York, N.Y. 10017

ISBN: 0-373-05419-X

First Silhouette Books printing April 1988

All the characters in this book are fictitious. Any
resemblance to actual persons, living or dead, is
purely coincidental.

SILHOUETTE, SILHOUETTE DESIRE and colophon
are registered trademarks of the publisher.

America's Publisher of Contemporary Romance

Printed in the U.S.A.

Books by Elaine Camp

Silhouette Romance

To Have, to Hold #99
Devil's Bargain #173
This Tender Truce #270

Silhouette Desire

Love Letters #207
Hook, Line and Sinker #251
Destiny's Daughter #298
Weathering the Storm #398
The Second Mr. Sullivan #419

Silhouette Special Edition

For Love or Money #113
In a Pirate's Arms #159
Just Another Pretty Face #263
Vein of Gold #285
Right Behind the Rain #301
After Dark #316

ELAINE CAMP

dreamed of becoming a writer for many years. Once she tried it she quickly became successful, perhaps due to her reporter's eye, which gives her a special advantage in observing human relationships.

To Nolan "Beau" Crowley
for his patient expertise.
You're a good friend and a great cousin.

—D.E.C.

One

"We've hired a detective."

Kelly Sullivan looked up from the fanfold pages on her desk. "You're joking," she accused, but then she remembered that joking was out of character for her boss. Joe Cauley's flushed, round face held not one hint of humor. "That is, I thought store security was on top of it."

"The shopping-mall executives decided to nip this in the bud before it gets completely out of hand. This credit-card thief has been working the mall for more than a month, and it's high time we put an end to his activities." Joe Cauley placed a fleshy hand on Kelly's desk. His forefinger tapped the Wysart Department Store letterhead at the top of the report Kelly was reading. "Our store's been hit hardest," he explained, then leaned forward for emphasis. "And the menswear department—*your* department—has the highest number of incidents."

"You're kidding," Kelly said, then wished she could kick herself. She didn't want her boss to think she was taking this lightly. "I know that several of my employees have been victims, but I had no idea that my department had been picked on more often."

"Well, now you know. You have twenty employees under you, and sixteen of them have reported irregular purchases made on their credit cards."

"What do you know." Kelly glanced at the report Cauley had given her about the credit-card scam being run in the Royal Conch Mall, the newest shopping center in St. Augustine, Florida. Why was the thief picking on her department? she wondered. Would it reflect poorly on her position as manager of the menswear department? "Mr. Cauley, I'm not being blamed for anything, am I?"

"Blamed?" Cauley shook his head in confusion. "I don't follow."

"I thought I heard an accusatory tone in your voice, but I don't see how any of this can be my fault. Granted, I'm responsible for this department, but I don't see how the credit-card scam is my responsibility."

"It's not." Cauley straightened, jerking his suit coat to correct its hang. "But I expect you to cooperate fully with the detective. He should be here any minute."

"Here?" She glanced around at her small, glass-walled office, which was situated at the center of the men's department. "I should straighten up."

"Why?" Cauley looked around at the limited space. "He's not coming here on a social call. He's going to ask you some questions and tour the department. It's business."

"Well, of course it's business," Kelly agreed, but couldn't stop herself from sweeping papers off the desk and into the drawers. "I'm a believer in first impressions, and I wouldn't want the detective to think I'm a slob. I run a tight ship, and my office should reflect that."

"Where the devil is he?" Cauley checked his expensive watch. "I've got other things to do than to wait around—oh, here he comes." Cauley stepped to the open door and motioned. "Over here, Sullivan."

Kelly started to join Cauley, then realized his last comment hadn't been for her but for the tall man approaching her office.

"Another Sullivan?" she asked her boss.

"Yes. Any relation?" he replied.

"Gosh, I hope not..." Her voice trailed away as the detective came forward to shake Joe Cauley's hand and then entered her office. She felt the color drain from her face and her knees shook as she forced herself to stand and greet the man who used to be her brother-in-law. "It's a small world," she said, surprising herself by speaking without the slightest tremor. She held out her hand to him and smiled. "Do you remember me, Beau?"

"Of course. I don't forget relatives." He shook her hand, and Kelly was impressed with his aplomb.

"Relatives?" Cauley broke in. "You two *are* related?"

"We used to be," Kelly explained. "I'm divorced from Beau's brother."

"Oh, I see." Cauley gave both Kelly and Beau a careful appraisal before he looked at his watch again. "Sullivan, Kelly will show you around the department. I'll leave you in her hands, if you don't mind."

"I don't mind in the least," Beau said with a smile that was both mischievous and sardonic.

"Good." Cauley gave a brief wave in Kelly's direction. "Carry on, then. I'm sure you'll have the thief in custody in no time, and then we can get on with our business."

"I'll do my best," Beau assured him, then slowly turned around to face Kelly when Joe Cauley had left. He studied her with green eyes that sparkled with pinpoints of light. "I'm sure Mother or Dad mentioned you were working here, but it slipped my mind until I saw your name on the employee list this morning."

"You just lost points with me," Kelly said, easing into her chair again, then motioning toward the other before she explained. "I was thinking you were unflappable, but you had an unfair advantage. Considering my handicap in not knowing the detective was you, I think I handled this well."

"Very well." He sat in the chair and drew out a leather notebook and gold pen from his jacket pocket. "How have you been?"

"Is this for the record?" Kelly asked, smiling as she looked at the notebook.

"No, just making small talk."

She started to answer him, but her nerves finally got the best of her and she was forced to drop her cool-as-a-cucumber persona. She laughed lightly at her poor play-acting, and shook her head when Beau looked puzzled at her reaction.

"I'm sorry, but I have to admit that I'm uncomfortable with this," she said, pushing back her chair and assuming a more relaxed posture. "I look at you, and I'm reminded of my marriage and my divorce and... well, it's difficult. Making small talk with you is like pulling teeth."

"Relax." He flipped the notebook shut and returned it and the pen to his pocket. He slanted one ankle on his other knee and lounged in the straight-backed chair. "I'm sorry this is uncomfortable for you. It shouldn't be. After all, we hardly know each other. I don't remember ever having a real conversation with you."

"You weren't around much," Kelly said, then paused a few moments for a quick assessment. His clothes were fashionable, but not trendy—gray suit, white shirt, foulard tie, black leather loafers. He had a lean body with a long waist and wide shoulders, so some tailoring was required for a perfect fit, she imagined. She realized that he'd noticed her careful scrutiny and was smiling at her with a hint of curiosity. "Nice tie," she said, covering for herself. "You'll have to forgive me. Working in menswear has taken its toll."

"You're forgiven." He ran a hand down his tie. "I bought this a few months ago in Bermuda."

"Still traveling around the world?" she asked, recalling the stories she'd heard from Ryan about his globe-trotting brother. "It seemed that every holiday, you were in a different part of the world. Indonesia, Mexico, Europe."

"Cleveland, Amarillo, Denver," he added with a grin. "I've spent most of my time in this country."

"I thought you were working with the FBI."

"I was, among other things. I've only recently acquired my private detective's license." He looked around. "How do you like working here?"

"I like it fine. I'm grateful for my job, and I mean to keep it."

His light green eyes widened, and he laid one hand against his chest in a gesture of shock. "I'm not after your job."

"I know." She laughed to herself at his misinterpretation. "I meant that I don't want this credit-card caper to damage my work record."

"How could it?" He took out the notebook and pen again. "Credit-card caper." He smiled and laughed silently. "Sounds like something out of a Hollywood script." He looked at her desk phone. "Could I make a quick call? I'm supposed to visit another store this morning, but I need to move that ahead to this afternoon."

"Go right ahead." Kelly pushed the telephone toward him, then sat back while he made his call.

There was little resemblance between Beau and Ryan. Both were redheads, but Ryan's hair was light, like butterscotch, while Beau's was a dark russet. Beau's eyes were wide and deep-set, and he had an attractive cleft in his chin and dimples in his cheeks. His nose was almost perfect, as if it had been carefully chiseled to a rounded tip. Unlike Ryan, he wasn't freckled. His skin was brown with the blush of a recent day in the sun.

No, he didn't physically resemble Ryan, and Kelly was glad of it. She didn't want to be reminded of Ryan day in and day out. Ryan was out of her life, and she wanted to keep it that way. The divorce had been traumatic, but almost three years had passed and Kelly liked herself better without Ryan Sullivan. She was stronger, more independent and definitely more productive than she had been during her ten-year marriage.

"Are you married yet?" Kelly asked when Beau had finished his phone call.

"No, not yet." He chuckled under his breath.

"What?" Kelly asked, wanting to be let in on the joke.

"Oh, nothing. I just wish I had a nickel for every time I've been asked that question."

Kelly shrugged apologetically. "Well, confirmed bachelors are a minority."

"I didn't say anything about being confirmed," he said as he flipped open his notebook.

"The Sullivan holdout," Kelly said with a teasing grin. "It must be a heavy burden to bear."

"I think Mother and Dad have given up on me. I'm always telling them that six married out of seven is quite an achievement. Besides, Ryan's had two wives, so I figure he's—" He stopped abruptly and glanced sheepishly at her. "I guess you heard that Ryan remarried."

"Yes, I heard. He sent me an announcement."

"He did?" His brows shot up, then he lowered them slowly. "Well, let's get back to our credit-card culprit, as you would probably put it. It seems he's been zeroing in on your department."

"You think the thief is a man?"

"Not necessarily. Could be a woman, but the purchases were more likely selected by a man."

"What purchases?" Kelly pulled up closer to the desk and craned forward to see his notes.

"Have there been any illegal purchases made on any of your credit cards?"

"No."

"And no one has reported their cards missing?"

"No, they just notice they're being billed for things they didn't buy. What purchases have been made?"

He checked the list. "Stereo, television, electric guitar, chain saw—"

"Women buy those things," Kelly interrupted a bit testily.

"Men's shirts, men's cologne, men's underwear," he went on with a pointed glance and a finishing smirk.

"A woman could be buying those things for her man," Kelly said in defense of her interpretation.

"Anything's possible. Why are you so sure it's a woman?"

"I'm not. I just think it's a little too early to rule out anything."

"Well, thanks, Sherlock. I'll keep that in mind."

His kidding sarcasm brought her up short and made her realize that she'd been overzealous.

"I'm sorry," she said, laughing at herself. "That sounded as if I was giving you advice, and heaven knows I wouldn't recognize a clue if it hit me right between the eyes."

When his eyes met hers and held fast, Kelly grew uncomfortable and was the first to look away. His directness had made her nervous. For a few moments she had thought that he was seeing her as something more than a former in-law. To counteract her discomfort, Kelly rose from the chair and moved toward the door.

"Mr. Cauley said that I should show you around the department, so where would you like to start?" she asked, trying to sound nonchalant.

"I'd like to start by asking you a few questions before we tour the plant," he said, stubbornly remaining in the chair. He twisted around to look at her. "Am I keeping you from something? I can come back later."

"No, it's just..." Kelly rolled her eyes at her predicament and went back to her chair. She pushed her curly black hair from her face and took a deep breath. "Like I said before, you make me nervous."

"You didn't say that before," he said. "You said you were uncomfortable, but you didn't say I made you nervous."

Kelly squinted one blue eye in a cagey expression. "What are you doing, writing down everything I say?"

"No, I have a good memory. It helps in this business."

She shrugged aside his comment. "Ask me the questions. Let's get this over with."

"It's not a formal inquisition, so relax."

"You keep saying that." She fidgeted under his green-eyed gaze and was grateful when he consulted his notebook.

"Sixteen of your employees have reported questionable purchases on their credit-card statements," he said, stating facts.

"That's right. It's all in this report." She tapped the neatly stacked document. "Security compiled it and sent one to each department manager."

"I've seen it," he said, clearly unimpressed. "So, someone is using the cards and putting them back before the owners realize they're missing."

"Right again." Kelly looked past him and spotted her assistant, Tamara Lane. She sent a silent plea to the other woman, and Tamara stopped just outside the office. Kelly answered a few more routine questions, then interrupted Beau's interrogation. "Excuse me, Beau, but let me introduce my assistant. Tamara Lane, this is Beau Sullivan. He's the detective who's been hired by the mall to track down the credit-card thief."

"Oh, really?" Tamara shook Beau's hand. "Nice to meet you. Your last name is Sullivan, too?"

"Yes." Beau glanced toward Kelly but made no attempt at any further explanation.

"Tamara, will you show Mr. Sullivan around the department?" Kelly sensed Beau's sharp glance, but hurried on. "I would, but I've got to finish up an inventory report before three."

"Sure, I don't mind." Tamara flung a hand toward the open door. "Where would you like to start?"

"I still have some questions for you, Kelly," Beau said pointedly.

"Can they wait until tomorrow or the next day?" Kelly begged off. "I didn't expect you, and I'm really swamped." She looked down at her uncluttered desk and wished she hadn't moved the hill of papers that had been there earlier.

"Shall I make an appointment?"

"No, don't be..." Kelly sat down again and consulted her desk calendar. "Well, maybe that would be better. Tomorrow at noon? I'll skip lunch and be at your mercy."

"No need for that," Beau said, starting for the door. "Lunch will be on me tomorrow. See you at noon."

"No, I..." Kelly looked up and realized she was talking to herself. Beau Sullivan was out of her office and heading toward the break room. Tamara shrugged and hurried after him. Kelly pressed her lips together into a line of irritation, then wondered if she wasn't creating a tempest in a teapot.

What's so terrible about answering a few questions posed by her ex-brother-in-law? she chided herself. It's not as if she were close to him. He was very nearly a stranger.

The Sullivan enigma, she thought, recalling her name for him that had always made Ryan laugh. The Sullivans were close-knit, but Beau was the wandering lamb who kept losing his way. Kelly had always thought that Beau's life sounded romantic, glamorous and like the stuff of daydreams. He'd worked as a policeman, for the treasury department and for the FBI. His life had sounded thrilling. He answered to no one.

Kelly released a dreamy sigh, wishing the same for herself. To answer to no one. To be independent. To live each day fully and positively. It sounded perfect. Maybe his independence would rub off on her. She might even learn from him how to be more self-sufficient.

She noted the lunch appointment on her calendar and promised herself she would be composed and not so jittery around him from then on. Beau was probably a crack detective, and with any luck he would apprehend the thief within days and then be gone. He never stayed around more than a day or two, she thought. By the end of the week he'd be nothing more than a memory.

"So how was your day?" Bette Zinquist asked, then took a sip of the tropical punch Kelly had handed her.

"Full of surprises," Kelly said, sliding into the rainbow-striped hammock suspended on her patio. She could smell the tangy ocean and hear the shrill call of gulls, so she paused a few moments to take it all in before she continued. "I told you about the credit-card thief?"

"Yes, the tricky devil. He's taking cards, making purchases, then putting the cards back before anyone notices they're missing."

"Right, and we can't catch him. He's hitting every store in the mall. Always employees, and his purchases are always made within the mall. But guess what."

"What?"

"My department is hardest hit."

"Uh-oh." Bette frowned, and creases formed between her eyebrows. "You're not going to take the blame for this, are you? Kelly, I thought you'd made progress. I thought you were through being the martyr, the victim."

"I am," Kelly said with a laugh. "I'm not taking this personally." She glanced at her next-door neighbor, saw that Bette wasn't completely convinced, and laughed again at her own weakness. "Well, for a few minutes I did take the blame. I let it get to me. In fact, I have this insane urge to try to catch the criminal myself, put the guy behind bars and make things right." Sensing Bette's disapproval, Kelly nodded and closed her eyes. The cry of gulls floated to her on a brisk ocean breeze.

When she'd moved to this house by the ocean, she'd met Bette and had sought her advice. Bette was everything Kelly had wanted to be: a free-spirited, unencumbered woman who lived life by her own rules and didn't take responsibility for every human being in her path. Through Bette's patient caring and understanding, Kelly had blossomed. Being divorced had ceased to be the worst thing that had ever happened to her. Bette was divorced and worked at an alligator farm, and Bette loved being single. She made a game of dating, instead of dreading every first date, as Kelly had done initially.

But old habits were hard to break, and Kelly knew she'd had a minor relapse when Joe Cauley had pointed out that the men's department at Wysart had been singled out.

"Kelly, you should leave the cops and robbers to the cops and robbers. Your job description doesn't include the apprehension of criminals," Bette pointed out in her droll, almost monotone voice. "What's Wysart going to do about this thief, just let him keep making monkeys out of everyone?"

"The mall hired a detective today," Kelly said, feeling a smile tip up one corner of her mouth.

"It's about time. Let *him* chase down the thief. The detective is male, right?"

"He's more than that."

"*More than male?* Good grief, what is he? Superman?"

Kelly turned her head to look at Bette, wanting to see the other woman's reaction. "He's my former brother-in-law."

Usually not given to overt reactions, Bette widened her eyes, and her mouth dropped open for a moment. "No kidding? That creates some interesting dilemmas." She tipped her brunette head to one side in a thoughtful pose. "And how do you feel about this, Kelly? Did you know him well while you were married?"

"Hardly at all," Kelly confessed.

"I always thought the Sullivans were as close as canned sardines."

"They are, with one exception. Beau is their wandering gypsy. He's single. The only single Sullivan man."

"Or woman, for that matter," Bette said. "Well, well. This is a fine mess, isn't it? Is this one older or younger than Ryan?"

"Older. The eldest, in fact."

"And, no doubt, he's a handsome son-of-a-gun."

"Why would you think that?" Kelly asked, shifting to her side and setting the hammock to swaying.

"Because I've seen three of the four brothers, and there wasn't an ugly one among them. Why should this one be any different?" Bette finished her fruit drink, then added, "Come to think of it, I might have met Beau." A thoughtful expression covered her face, then she gave a sharp nod. "I think Beau was a sophomore in high school when I was a senior. How old is he?"

"Around thirty-six, I guess."

"Yes, that's about right. I'm forty. I vaguely remember him. He was on the basketball team. Made varsity in his sophomore year."

"All the Sullivan men are athletic," Kelly said, thinking of Ryan's numerous football, baseball and swimming trophies she'd dusted more times than she cared to remember.

"Has he settled in St. Augustine, or is he passing through it again?" Bette asked.

"I don't know." Kelly flopped onto her back and stared at the sky, which was growing darker by the minute as dusk approached. "We didn't talk much. I was so rattled, I turned him over to my assistant and made myself scarce."

"Chicken," Bette accused, then made some clucking noises.

Kelly laughed, nodding enthusiastically. "I admit it. But I was caught completely off guard. He, on the other hand, knew I was working there. I hate it when I'm at a disadvantage. Tomorrow will be different."

"You're seeing him again tomorrow?" Bette asked with a sly grin.

"Please don't put it that way."

"What way?"

"Like it's a date or something. I have an appointment with him to discuss the stealing that's going on right under my nose. Ooh, it makes me furious!" She pounded her fists into the hammock's canvas. "I should have noticed something, seen someone, been able to catch the guy in the act!"

"Take it easy, Sherlock," Bette said dryly.

Kelly smiled. "That's the second time today I've been called that. I'm sure that Beau will catch the crook within a day or two and my troubles will be over."

"How did he act around you? Was he polite or hostile?"

"Polite. Why should he be hostile?"

"Some family members take a divorce personally and treat the former in-law like a blight."

"No, he's not like that. He was very understanding of the situation."

"So why did you become unglued?"

"Oh, I don't know. Because...because I'm me." Kelly flapped her hands in a helpless gesture. Laughing, she swung out of the hammock. "Show me a Sullivan, then show me the door...quick!"

Bette laughed with her as they moved from the patio to inside Kelly's house. A lamp cast a soft glow over the modest dining room and kitchen, which were separated by a free-standing counter that housed the stove and provided enough space for two place settings.

"I've got to get home," Bette said, rinsing out her glass and putting it in the dishwasher. "Some people from a nature magazine are coming to the farm tomorrow to do an article."

"How's business at the croc farm?"

"It's a gator farm. We only have five crocs," Bette corrected with a feigned scowl. "And you know it."

"Alligators, crocodiles. What's the difference?"

"A big difference. Crocs have tapering snouts and—" Bette cut off her explanation and shook a finger at Kelly. "You know how to get me going, don't you? Speaking of going, I am. Good luck with Beau Sullivan tomorrow."

"Thanks. I'll need it."

"Ask him if he remembers me from high school." At the front door, Bette turned back toward Kelly. "I took a course in self-confidence once, and the instructor said that if you ever feel ill at ease or defenseless, just imagine that the other person is nude. It's suppose to make you feel superior or something. Think that would help?"

Kelly considered the suggestion, then burst out laughing. "No, not in this case. I think that's the *last* thing I should do."

"Yes, well, you're probably right." Bette delivered a mocking frown. "Especially with *your* wild imagination."

"Get out of here," Kelly said, still laughing as she playfully shoved her best friend out the door and locked it behind her.

Two

On Tuesday morning, pedestrian traffic was light at the Royal Conch Mall as Beau Sullivan strode confidently along the wide center corridor. On either side of him were specialty shops that displayed a variety of merchandise from giant chocolate-chip cookies to Waterford crystal. He carried a briefcase stuffed with reports concerning the credit-card thief, but his thoughts weren't on thieves or other sordid business.

He could see the Wysart sign ahead of him, delicate wine-colored letters formed by a calligraphist against a cream background. The department store was what the mall business called an anchor. Because of its importance, it occupied a choice position at one end of the mall.

Beau smiled to himself as he stepped over the threshold and into the world of Wysart. He'd spoken to his parents last night and had told them that he would be having lunch with their former daughter-in-law.

"How does she look?" his mother had asked with genuine concern.

"She looks great. Really great," he'd assured her with genuine enthusiasm.

"I heard that she's doing well in her job," his father had said.

"Yes, she's manager of the menswear department."

"Menswear?" his father had echoed with some confusion. "Why would they put a woman over that? It's a messed-up world, and that proves it."

"Dad, men dress for women. I think it makes perfect sense."

"You would. Kelly would be better off selling dishes or vacuums. She was always a good housekeeper."

"That she was," his mother had agreed. "Never was in her house that it wasn't spotless. And cook! That lass could make beans and franks a new experience."

He chuckled to himself at the remembered conversation, then walked into the men's department. He spotted Kelly by a rack of twenty-five-percent-off sports jackets. She was with a customer, so Beau watched as she conducted the sale. She was charming without being artificial, friendly without being flirtatious. The customer seemed comfortable with her.

Beau knew the feeling. He was at ease around her with none of the usual getting-to-know-you awkwardness that went along with first encounters. He particularly liked her frequent smile. It was always there, lurking in her midnight-blue eyes or at the corners of her mouth, ready to spring forth and dazzle. And he loved her laugh. Full throated and lusty. No giggles, no twitters. It was an honest-to-goodness laugh, totally unpretentious and unpracticed. She was a woman of good humor. That had been evident from the outset. Funny how he'd never noticed that about her in their earlier, brief meetings at his family home. For the life of him, he could recall little about her from the past. She'd blended into the wallpaper. She had been Ryan's wife, and beyond that Beau could remember nothing about her.

Of course, he was a stranger to most of his brothers- and sisters-in-law. Maybe that would change now that he'd decided to stay put in St. Augustine for a while, he thought.

For once he was glad not to have been around much the past dozen years, because his impression of Kelly Sullivan was unsullied by her former association with him, however inconsequential. He was a man who relied heavily on first impressions, and Kelly impressed him. He sensed her dedication, drive and perseverance, all of which he admired. Kelly Sullivan was a go-getter, just like him.

Beau smiled with appreciation, then folded his arms across his chest and leaned back against a table of dress shirts. Kelly took a pale yellow sports jacket from her customer and turned in the direction of the cash register. She saw Beau and her steps faltered momentarily, but she was quick to recover.

"Be right with you," she called to him, then escorted her customer to the register island.

As Beau watched her complete the transaction, he decided that if lunch went well, he'd ask her out for dinner. She'd probably turn him down flat, but he was a sucker for a challenge, and rejection reinforced his determination. In an unconscious movement, he straightened the knot of his striped tie, then slid his hand down the front of his blue shirt to press out any wrinkles. He strode forward, wishing he'd worn dress slacks instead of jeans.

"I'm afraid I'm a few minutes early," he said, stopping on the other side of the counter. "If you're busy, I can wait."

"No need for that." She held up a finger. "Wait right there while I get my purse."

"Okay." He turned to watch her cross to her office. She had a nice figure, just past slim but a long way from plump. Her trim white skirt and jacket, coral-colored blouse, and gold earrings and necklace enhanced her tanned skin and ebony hair. She returned, carrying a white clutch purse and bestowing on him one of her terrific smiles that made him feel all gooey inside.

"Do you want to eat here at the mall?" she asked.

"That depends. Is that cafeteria any good?"

She wrinkled her nose in distaste. "Not really. But the Gold Pearl serves up great salads and sandwiches."

"Sounds good. Let's go." He placed a hand at her elbow and was pleased when she didn't pull away from his courtesy as they took the escalator to the second-level restaurant.

They were shown to a table and given menus. Kelly ordered a seafood salad, and Beau decided to try the lobster bisque. Kelly kept up a light-hearted conversation that centered on the exasperation of dealing with the public. Her stories about some of her more perplexing customers amused him, and he was sorry when their lunches arrived and Kelly grew silent.

The lobster bisque was creamy and rich, but he hardly noticed, since his attention was riveted on Kelly. She had the most animated face he'd ever seen. When she talked, her facial expressions filled in the spaces of her story and said what she couldn't speak of in mixed company. Her eyes, a dark royal blue, sparkled and twinkled and teased. Her lips, moist and full, had a language all their own, as did her finely shaped brows, which she arched and lowered, sometimes together and sometimes separately.

She had a small head set on a long, graceful neck. Her black hair fell to her shoulders in a profusion of loose curls and was held back on either side by ivory combs. Wispy bangs stopped just shy of her eyebrows.

"How's your salad?" he asked for want of anything better to say.

"What salad?" She pushed aside her empty plate. "I love good food, and that was one good salad." She rested her rounded chin in her hands and gazed openly across the table at him. "I thought we were going to discuss the credit-card thief."

He spooned the last of the bisque into his mouth, then nodded when the waitress came to clear the table. "How about dessert?"

"No, thanks. But I would accept a cup of coffee."

"Two coffees, please," Beau ordered, then realized that Kelly wore an expectant expression. "Ah, yes. The thief."

"That *is* why we met for lunch, isn't it?"

"Well..." He looked at her from beneath his lowered brows and wondered if he should tell the truth. "Yes, I guess so, but I also wanted to get to know you. I missed my earlier chance."

"Earlier..." She pressed her lips together when she caught his drift. "Oh, right." She shrugged suddenly. "Don't feel any obligation, Beau. I'm no longer in your family, and you don't have to—"

"I know, but that's not what I meant. Your company isn't an obligation. It's a pleasure."

She laughed, all husky and suggestive. Beau felt a smile curve his mouth and his neck grew warm inside his shirt collar. What was it about her that made his heart leap and his insides quiver? It wasn't just a physical attraction. It was deep, like a tremor in the very core of him.

"You Sullivan men," she said, still laughing and shaking a tapered finger at him. "You've all had intimate contact with the Blarney stone. Making any progress with catching our thief? I'll be glad when you nab him. Things will get back to normal, and I can relax."

It took him a moment to follow her lightning-quick turn of conversation. He gleaned from it that she was uncomfortable with flattery, or was she only uncomfortable when it was delivered by a Sullivan? The waitress brought the coffee and the check, which Beau paid with a credit card.

"Credit cards are a pain, aren't they?" Kelly commented, then rushed on before he could offer a viewpoint. "Right after my divorce I was advised that I should establish credit in my own name. I applied for credit cards and was turned down by most of the companies, so—"

"Turned down? Why?" Beau interrupted.

She gave him a look she probably saved for blithering idiots. "Because I'm a divorced woman, of course."

"That's discrimination."

"That's life," she said in a jaded tone. "At least that's life for now. Maybe in the future things will be different, especially as the divorce rate climbs and women are promoted into the inner circles of business and finance." She sipped the hot coffee before picking up the thread of conversation. "I was sent a few cards and I established credit. Boy, did I establish credit!" She laughed, throwing back her head and making Beau grin from ear to ear. She had beautiful teeth, straight and glistening, with the merest hint of an overbite. "I went to a financial counselor to get my act together."

"And you learned your lesson?"

"And how," she agreed. "I never charge unless it's an emergency."

"Not even at Christmas?"

"Especially not at Christmas. I put money aside each month in a Christmas account so that I have plenty by the time Thanksgiving rolls around."

"Smart woman," Beau said, nodding his approval. "We should all be so fiscally responsible."

"You're not?"

He replaced his credit card in his wallet with a wry smile. "Not always. I tend to be overly generous where loved ones are concerned."

She studied him for a few moments before murmuring, "If that's your worst fault, you can rest easy."

He decided he should offer something professional so that she wouldn't think he was all talk and no action.

"When I was in the break room, I noticed that you don't have lockers."

"That's right."

"Where do your employees keep their purses?"

"On that table in the corner of the room, or in my office."

"You lock them up in your office?"

"No. I have a safe in there, but it's not large enough to hold handbags. You think we should begin locking things up, right? Well, tell it to management. I asked for lockers when I first got here, and that's as far as it went."

"Lockers are the logical solution."

"I know, I know." She narrowed her eyes in a fit of irritation. "But since when is management logical? They put security on this, and those guys lurked around trying to catch the thief in the act. I mean, I don't know who's taking the cards, but whoever he is, he's not a raving idiot. He knows a security guard when he sees one, and he's not going to lift a card while a guy wearing a gun strapped around his middle is watching him." She looked pointedly at Beau's jacket, at a place just under his left arm. "Do you carry a gun?"

"Sometimes, but not there." He flattened his left hand against the right side of his chest. "Here. I'm left-handed."

"So am I!" She seemed immensely pleased, but then her mood changed with the blink of an eye from pleasure to concern. "You're not carrying a gun now, are you?"

"No, I figured I wouldn't need one with you. I pegged you for the type who'd come along peacefully, especially since I'm paying."

She delivered a cagey smile that sent his heart into a somersault. "Right. I never pass up a free lunch."

"Good. Then let's do this again tomorrow." He threw down his napkin with a decisive flourish. "I'll be by around noon and—"

"Sorry. Tomorrow is my day off."

"Even better. Where do you live? I'll pick you up and we'll—"

"I've already made other plans." She tossed her napkin onto the table with an even more decisive flourish. "I've got to get back to the salt mines. Thanks for lunch, and good luck with your investigation. The sooner you catch the thief, the better."

"Let me walk back with you."

"No, don't bother. I'm stopping off at the credit-union office first. Give my regards to your parents. 'Bye now."

He barely had enough time to rise up from his chair before she was off and running. He lifted a hand in a useless farewell, waving lamely at her back.

"Well, well," he muttered under his breath. "So much for the Sullivan charm."

* * *

"If I didn't know better, I'd say that he was coming on to me," Kelly said, toying with a pencil instead of looking across the desk at Tamara Lane.

"That's great."

"Great?" Kelly repeated incredulously, lifting her gaze to confront Tamara's shining emerald eyes. "It's not great. It's... it's annoying."

"Since when is attention from a gorgeous man annoying?" Tamara chided as she propped her feet on top of Kelly's desk.

Kelly was momentarily disconcerted by the sight of the white boots with red stitching. She examined the rest of Tamara's outfit—denim skirt, western-style shirt, neckerchief—and shook her head in a baffled way.

"What is this?" she asked with a flick of her hand. "Your tribute to Will Rogers?"

"It's my western ensemble," Tamara said, pronouncing the last word with a French accent. "Wait until you see my jungle theme. I might wear it tomorrow."

"I can hardly wait," Kelly said, smiling although her tone was richly sardonic. "I hope it's not a gorilla suit."

Tamara laughed with good humor, then furrowed her brow in mock seriousness. "Back to important business. What did Beau Sullivan do that made you think he was trying to score points?"

"It wasn't so much what he did," Kelly explained. "He asked me to lunch again, and this time he made no pretense of it being a business lunch."

"Sounds promising."

"Quit that! I don't want his attentions."

"Why not?" Tamara asked, flinging out her hands dramatically.

Kelly threw down the pencil and angled forward, arms crossed upon the desk. "Because he's my ex-husband's brother."

"Yeah, so?"

Kelly rolled her eyes in an appeal for more powerful assistance. "So, his coming on to me isn't proper."

"Get real, Kelly. He's not a blood relation. There's nothing wrong with him being interested in you."

"Maybe not in the strict sense, but it's uncomfortable for me."

"Is he a lot like your ex?"

"No."

"When you were married was Beau interested in you then, too?"

"Heavens, no!" Kelly laughed at the notion. "I hardly ever saw him. I gathered that he wasn't interested in cultivating family ties."

"He's interested now." Tamara wiggled her brows suggestively.

"I shouldn't have mentioned it to you," Kelly said, grabbing up her purse and rising from the chair. "You take things to the extreme." She smiled and glanced around, making sure she had everything. "I'm off. The men's department is all yours."

"Gee, thanks." Tamara's boots met the floor as she reached for the buzzing telephone. "Have a good evening."

Kelly hurried from the office, anxious to leave her work behind and get home to a cool shower and a cold roast-beef sandwich. The sun was shining brightly, and it was warmer than usual for September in St. Augustine. It felt more like July, and Kelly was glad she'd parked her Mustang in the covered parking lot. Still, it was like a furnace inside the car. Kelly fumbled with the ignition key, anxious to start the engine and the air conditioner, but the engine didn't respond. Kelly tried again, her heart sinking at the ominous *click, click* of the ignition as it failed to make contact with the battery.

"Don't do this to me," she warned the car. "Not today. Not when it's a hundred degrees in here!"

She tried again, but there was still no response from the engine. She applied the flat of her hand to the steering wheel in a vicious slap, then spotted a man standing opposite her car. His stance was arrogantly relaxed, ankles and arms crossed as he leaned back against the fender of a black Corvette. Kelly released her breath in a long sigh of exasperation as Beau Sullivan straightened from his lounging position and came forward with a confident, long-legged stride. He bent at the waist to look inside the car at her.

"Trouble in River City?"

His reference to *The Music Man* made her smile, and the tune from it floated through her head.

"Yes, sir, we've got trouble," she said, almost chanting the lines from the song. "It starts with *T* and that rhymes with *B*, and that stands for 'battery.'"

He snapped his fingers and chuckled as he went around to the front of the car and lifted the hood.

"Do you have jumper cables?" Kelly asked, sticking her head out the window.

"No, not on me."

"Then how are you going to get it started?" She stared at the pocketknife he exhibited. "With that?"

"With this. Your cables are corroded. I'll scrape off the stuff and you should get a charge."

"I don't want a charge, but my car could use one," Kelly smarted off without thinking, then shrugged when Beau peered around the raised hood to scowl playfully at her. "Sorry. Couldn't help myself."

"Give it a try."

She turned the key, not for a moment believing that the car would start. When it did she let out a whoop of joy.

"You're a genius," she declared as she flipped up the air-conditioning switch. "Handiest man with a pocket-knife I've ever met."

He folded the knife and dropped it back into his pocket. "You owe me."

The way he said it made her catch her breath. She regarded him from the corner of her eye and thought that his smile was predatory.

"Will you take cash or a check?" she joked, feeling her skin tingle and wishing she could stop it.

"Dinner."

"Rain check?"

He shook his head and rested the heels of his hands against the top of the door frame.

"I was looking forward to a cool shower, a quick dinner and a quiet evening alone," she confessed, hoping he'd back off.

"I'll come by around seven. That will give you time to shower."

She stared straight ahead at the Corvette and weighed her options. She could tell him to get lost. She could laugh and tell him to get serious. She could surrender for the moment and be gracious.

"Look, if you really don't want to go out, then forget it," he said, shoving himself away from the car. "I happen to enjoy your company and I thought..." He stared at his shoes, positively crestfallen. "Oh, never mind."

"Seven? Did you say seven?" she asked, and when he smiled, her heart slipped loose of his moorings and floated in her chest.

"Yes. Seven."

"I'll be ready," she said, surprised by her acceptance. "I live on Anastasia. You know where that is?"

"Yes. Just outside the city."

"Right. It's the Oceanside housing division, and my house is on Sandpiper Avenue. Number 609."

"Got it."

"Are you sure? I can write it down."

"No, that's okay. I know the area. I'm staying a few miles up the highway from you."

"That so?" She filed this away with some qualms. "Well, thanks for getting my car started. I'll see you later."

"Later." He winked and stood back from her car.

Kelly swallowed hard, willing herself not to wink back at him. Why did he have to be so attractive? she wondered miserably as she drove from the shaded lot into the bright sunlight.

When she arrived home, she showered quickly and then spent an hour trying on and discarding outfits. She finally selected a lime-green blouse and khaki walking shorts, allowing for the uncommonly hot weather. She stepped into leather sandals while she fastened pearl studs to her earlobes. She was all atremble, and it galled her.

"What's wrong with you?" she demanded of her reflection in the dresser mirror. Her cheeks were flushed, and her eyes were bright with a fever she hadn't felt in years. "You're going to dinner with Beau Sullivan. Big deal. There's nothing wrong with it. Just be nice, courteous, friendly. Treat him as you would an old acquaintance." She moved closer to the mirror to apply lipstick.

What was there about him that made her breathless? she wondered as she steadied her hand enough to color her lips with the tiny brush. Was it only his bloodline, or was there more to it? Could it be that her femininity responded to his masculinity? She shook her head, denying the thought but acknowledging its origins. He was good-looking with a latent sensuality that appealed to her.

Since her divorce she hadn't met too many men she'd give a second look, so she found this preoccupation unusual. She sprayed cologne across her inner arms and along the sides of her neck, then stepped back to examine the results. At that moment the doorbell chimed, and she jumped all over, then a shiver coursed through her. Irritated by her fluttering nerves, she marched from the bedroom to the front door. Throwing it open, she forced a cheery smile to her lips even as a groan resounded in her mind. Why did he have to look so damned good? she wondered. She grabbed up her purse and stepped outside, not inviting him in, because she didn't want him invading her life any more than was necessary.

"I'm ready and I'm hungry," she said brightly. "Did you pick out a restaurant?"

"I thought we might go to the Floating Fish," he said, glancing at the closed door before he fell into step beside her.

"Great choice." She examined the black sports car. "This is the one that was in the garage. The one you were leaning on."

"That's right."

"Rental?"

"No, it's mine." He opened the passenger door for her. "I washed it just for you."

"How thoughtful," she said, joining in with his light jesting. She sat on one hip and leaned against the door, allowing lots of space between her and Beau Sullivan. While he was busy executing a U-turn, Kelly admired the fit of his army-green shorts and yellow knit shirt. "I'm glad you dressed casually," she said.

"In this heat, a tuxedo is out of the question." He glanced her way. "I entertained the thought of bringing flowers, but I decided you'd get all flustered and make more out of it than you should."

"Is that so?" she said, crossing her arms and giving him a smile of cocky self-assurance. "You think you've got my number, don't you?"

"I'm good at reading people. For instance, right now I sense that you're as nervous as a sixteen-year-old on prom night."

She released a spate of laughter, although she was unnerved by his ability to see through her. "I am not! Why should I be nervous?"

"Why, indeed?" He shrugged aside the subject. "There are more tourists than there used to be during the fall."

"Yes, it's a year-round business now," she agreed, thankful he'd changed the subject. "Being the oldest city in America used to be our only draw, but we've expanded into the museum business. Oh, and let's not forget the Fountain of Youth."

"Right. What museums?" he asked, steering the car across the bridge that connected Anastasia Island with St. Augustine.

"Wax and curious artifacts."

"Oh, those." He smiled, looking around at the familiar and unfamiliar. "I heard that they charge admission to the beaches now."

"Yes, but only during the summer. Come September, no admission fee."

He parked the car behind the restaurant and laughed under his breath when she scrambled out before he could assist her. At the steps leading up to the floating restaurant, he placed five fingertips against the small of her back.

"Why do I get the feeling that you want to keep me at arm's length?" he asked in a voice that reminded her of aged brandy—smooth and full-bodied.

She tossed her head, flinging her hair back over her shoulders. "I give up. Why?"

He laughed good-naturedly, then told the hostess that he'd like a table for two by the windows. The hostess seated them, handed them menus and said she'd send over the waiter. They ordered white wine coolers to sip while they studied the extensive menu. Refills were required before Kelly finally settled on crabmeat crepes and Beau on fisherman's stew and corn bread.

"How long are you planning to stay in St. Augustine?" Kelly asked while they waited for their dinners.

"A long time, I hope. I opened my own detective agency and joined the chamber of commerce." He laughed at her reaction. "Kelly, you're staring at me as if I've sprouted an extra nose."

"Sorry, I'm just flabbergasted. Beau Sullivan is settling down? It's outrageous, almost sacrilegious. Don't you know how many people live vicariously through you? While I was married the Sullivans were always updating your life of danger and adventure. We were all secretly jealous of you."

"That's ironic," he said, moving the pads of his fingers through the condensation on his stemmed glass.

"Why?"

"Oh... nothing." He squared his shoulders as if throwing off a dark mood. "Is this the only job you've held since your divorce?"

"You've got to be kidding," she accused, then noticed the innocence behind his eyes. "Beau, do you really think I started as manager of a department with no previous experience?"

"No, of course not. But is Wysart the only place you've worked?"

"No. I was a hostess at a restaurant for a few months, then I got a job as a secretary with an insurance company, but I didn't like that, so I quit. I worked with a temporary secretarial service for a month or so before Wysart hired me."

"And you worked your way up the ladder," he added.

"That's right. I started in housewares, got transferred to gifts and then to menswear. Not here, though."

"Not here?"

"No, in Miami."

"I didn't know you'd lived there."

"I moved there after the divorce was final. I couldn't find a job here, so I sold the house and headed for the big city."

"It must have been tough at first."

She nodded and looked away from his sympathetic expression. "Yes, it was the worst time in my life. I didn't know who I was or what I wanted. I was adrift. It was frightening." An undulating wave shifted the floating restaurant noticeably, and Kelly laughed. "It felt a lot like this," she said, grabbing the edge of the table in an exaggerated gesture of panic. She looked out the window to the bank of thunderheads on the horizon. "No wonder it was so humid today. It looks as if it's going to rain buckets."

Beau followed her eye line. "Maybe this restaurant was a bad idea."

"Don't worry. We'll be finished and on our way home before those clouds make their way to us." She folded her hands in her lap and leaned back in her chair when the waiter approached and placed their steaming selections on the table. Kelly tasted the crepe and rolled her eyes in ecstasy. "How's yours?"

"Delicious," Beau assured her. "You said you were frightened once you were on your own," he said after sampling a generous wedge of corn bread. "What scared you?"

"Everything. I'd never slept alone in a house. For the first few months, I didn't get one full night of sleep. Not one." She shook her head, recalling those terrible nights when every sound, however common, threatened her sanity. "I married right out of high school, so I moved from my parents' home to my husband's home."

"Husband's home," he repeated with a quirky smile. "Your home, too, wasn't it?"

"Yes, but it didn't feel that way at first. He was paying for it. I just decorated it and kept it clean."

"That's an odd way to look at it," Beau said, clearly baffled by her attitude.

"That's the way I felt *at first*," she repeated. "You see, your brother picked out the house and surprised me. Later on we moved into a place of *our* choosing, not just his."

"And you felt as if the new house was yours."

"Yes." She shrugged. "It probably sounds silly to you, but women understand when I tell them." She waved her fork, signaling a return to her original subject. "Anyway, independence was scary to me, but now it's what keeps me going." She glanced covertly at him from beneath her thick lashes. "I envy your life-style. Someday—-someday I'll be footloose, like you."

He regarded her with a fierce intensity for a few moments before averting his gaze. Kelly was left with a feeling that she'd escaped, but from what, she wasn't sure. She devoted her attention to the carefully prepared meal but was agonizingly conscious of every move Beau made. She noticed that his lashes were sable and created a beautiful frame for his green eyes, and that his hands were long fingered, with veins running along the backs of them. Cords of veins ran up the inside of his arms, where the skin was only lightly suntanned. After a fleeting study of the way his knit shirt fit snugly across his chest, Kelly surmised that Beau Sullivan had not one extra ounce of fat on him. Her gaze slipped further down. Not even a spare tire, she surmised. The last time she'd seen her ex-husband, which had been in the judge's quarters following the divorce hearing, she'd noted that Ryan was getting thick around the middle.

"How's Ryan doing these days?" she asked, shocking herself almost as much as she'd shocked Beau. He almost choked on his food. "Forget I asked. I don't know what possessed me to—"

"No problem," Beau assured her, coughing a little and waving one hand to waylay her. He reached for his water glass, from which he drank deeply. "I'm just surprised you brought him up. I'd already decided that his name was taboo around you."

"Don't be silly," she said, scoffing. "I don't despise him or anything. In fact, I hardly ever give him a thought. Being with you, of course, brings him to mind."

"Yes, well, he's doing fine, and I wish I didn't bring him to your mind. I was hoping you'd see me for myself—by myself—and not as one in a family package."

"Why is that so important to you?"

"Because I don't look at you and see only my brother's former wife," he answered sharply.

"What *do* you see?" Kelly asked before she could stop herself.

He looked at her fully, eye to eye and unblinking. It was that same fierce look that had so unnerved her, but she forced herself not to show him how much. "I see a beautiful woman, whom I would very much enjoy getting to know better." He chuckled when she blushed. "You asked. Kelly, wouldn't you like to see me again?"

"Socially?" she asked, barely getting the word out without stuttering.

"Yes."

"I...I don't know." She took a long drink of wine to steady her nerves. "I suppose we could be friends."

His eyes laughed uproariously at her, although his smile was merely polite. "Well, that's a start." He looked around to catch the waiter's eye. "Dessert?"

"Not for me." She had suddenly lost all interest in food. She looked out the window again at the towering clouds. "We should leave now if we want to outrun the rainstorm."

"Okay." He paid the check, then helped her from her chair. When they were outside, he sniffed the air. "I can smell the rain."

"So can I," Kelly said, breathing deeply as they crossed the parking lot to his car. "You're not staying with your parents?" she asked when they were both settled in the leather bucket seats.

"When have I ever been known to stay with my parents?"

She laughed, realizing he was right. "Well, did you rent an apartment?"

Before he could answer, a gust of wind shook the car, then another. The trees along the highway were bent double. Beau gripped the steering wheel and kept the car on the ribbon of highway.

"Good grief!" Kelly laid one hand against her heart, feeling its frantic kick. "Think we'll make it to my place before all hell breaks loose?"

"My timing is usually pretty good." He pressed down on the accelerator, exceeding the speed limit for the next two miles. When he pulled into her driveway, a few fat drops splattered on the windshield. "My timing is holding up."

"It sure is." Kelly wrenched open the door and turned to tell him not to bother seeing her to the door, but she was too late. He was already out of the car. She ran across the lawn and up onto the porch with Beau at her heels. "You'd better go before the storm hits." She looked at the sky, which had turned pewter. Rain clouds raced across the gray background, pushed by mighty wind gusts. Kelly shivered and reached out to open the storm door. "It really looks bad. I wouldn't want you to get caught in the middle of it." She fumbled for her door key.

He reached out and covered her hand, closing her fingers around her brass key ring. "Thanks for going out with me."

"It was nice." She sensed him moving closer, then realized that he was angling his head for a kiss. Kelly jerked back and felt her eyes widen as alarm bolted through her.

"What?" Beau asked, laughing at her reaction. "I was just going to kiss you."

"I...that's what I thought." She extracted her hand from his and unlocked the front door.

"And what's wrong with that?" Beau persisted, holding open the storm door and leaning into her even as she shrank back from him. "Kelly, answer me."

"You're right. I overreacted." She smiled in concession, then stood on tiptoe and kissed the dimple in his left cheek. "Now, shake a leg, before the storm—"

He reached for her with his free hand, his fingers clutching the side of her blouse and hauling her closer. Kelly's breath whistled down her throat in a gasp when Beau covered her slack lips with his firm mouth. His lips were cool, but heated quickly against hers. His kiss was hard and unrelenting. It rattled her, threw her completely off guard. She wasn't sure if it were thunder she heard or just her own racing pulse. She pressed a fist against his shoulder and was relieved when the pressure of his mouth lessened, but the respite was only momentary as he merely wrapped his arm around her waist and sought her mouth again.

This kiss, however, was delightfully different, showing infinite expertise. He was kissing her *the old-fashioned way*, she thought with a little moan of surrender as her resistance melted with each gentle nudge of his mouth. She had expected to feel the thrust of his tongue, but he kept the kiss straightforward, traditional—the kind Kelly had thought men had discarded in the sixties. It was a revelation to find a man who still remembered how sweet a kiss could be if executed properly.

She knew that if his second kiss had been something less sensuous and more sexual, she would have forced him away from her. She guessed that he knew this, too, because he continued his incessant nudging and nibbling until Kelly wondered if she might collapse in his arms.

When he did straighten from her, his eyes held a glimmer of sheer pleasure that made Kelly's stomach muscles flutter.

"There, that wasn't so bad, was it?" he asked, then turned abruptly and bounded off the porch.

The sky opened up. Rain fell, slanting sideways like wind-tossed sheets. Beau sought refuge in his car, and he didn't even glance in Kelly's direction as he reversed from the driveway and sent the sleek sports car speeding along the residential street. Kelly stood for a long time in the doorway and watched the rainstorm while a storm of a different sort raged within her.

When she did go inside, she felt as if she were floating instead of walking. It was a dangerous feeling, a voice in her head warned. He's Ryan's brother, for crying out loud!

Kelly fell backward onto her bed, a satisfied smile spreading over her tingling lips. He doesn't kiss like Ryan, she thought. In fact, he didn't kiss like any man she'd ever met before. She wondered what other unique qualities he possessed.

Three

Kelly watched the eighteen-year-old across the desk from her. Julie Scott fidgeted in the chair and twisted a strand of her brown hair around one finger. She chewed her gum furiously, revealing how anxious she was at being called into Kelly's office. The young woman's expectant expression and timid smile didn't make Kelly's task any easier.

Kelly opened a folder and glanced down at the report inside it. Dread seized her, and she felt her palms grow damp and her breathing shallower.

"I'm glad you asked me in here," Julie said, twisting in the chair as she crossed one slim leg over the other. "I was wondering if I could get in a few extra hours over the Labor Day holiday. I'm staying in town instead of going to Tampa with my friends."

Kelly drew a deep breath and looked squarely at the young woman. "I don't think so, Julie. In fact, I'm afraid this will be your last day here."

"Wh-what?" Julie swallowed her gum. "Don't I get two weeks' notice or something?"

"Not in this case." Kelly tapped the folder with the end of her pen. "This is a security report about you."

Julie strained forward, trying to see the document. "What does it say?"

"It says you've been giving your friends unauthorized discounts." Kelly handed over the single sheet. "You may read it, if you want."

Julie's eyes filled with tears as she read the report. "This is a lie."

"Julie, please," Kelly said, then took the report back and slipped it into the file folder. "We have sales slips and register receipts. We even have a statement from one of your friends that bears out the accusation."

"Which one ratted on me?"

"Does it matter?" Kelly asked with a sad smile. "Julie, you're a smart girl. You knew what you were doing was illegal."

"And you're firing me over this? Look, I'll pay back the money Wysart lost." She rolled her eyes. "As if Wysart needs it. This place is making money hand over fist."

"First of all, Wysart didn't *lose* money. The money was *stolen* by you," Kelly said, trying hard to keep her voice steady. "Also, you shouldn't bite the hand that feeds you. Wysart management, at this time, has decided not to press charges against you."

"Charges? You mean, they were thinking of arresting me?"

"Why so shocked?" Kelly asked, shocked herself to see that the younger woman had no idea of the severity of her actions. "Julie, stealing, in whatever form, is illegal. Yes, it's a crime. In lieu of pressing charges, Wysart is willing to let you go without recommendation, which will be a black spot on your work record. But don't push your luck by bad-mouthing the company, or the company might just change its mind. You don't want that, Julie."

"No, I guess not." Julie sniffed and wiped tears from her eyes. "So I'm canned?"

"Yes, and you're also lucky. I've worked for companies that would have shown you no mercy." Kelly stood and extended one hand. "Good luck, Julie. I'm not going to deliver a sermon, but I will say that I sincerely hope you've learned something from this."

"Thanks." Julie barely touched her hand, then whirled and left the office, head bent, arms pumping.

Kelly lifted a derisive brow and released a sigh of relief, glad that the confrontation she'd been dreading all day was over. She went over the security report again and stared at the final signature, which was written in a clear, bold script: B. P. Sullivan. Kelly shook her head, wondering when Beau had been lurking around during the past four days. She sure hadn't seen him.

Kelly caught sight of her assistant and motioned her to come inside and close the door. "Tamara, come on in. Sit down."

"Uh-oh," Tamara said with false concern. "Does this mean I'm the next one on your hit list?"

"It's not my list. It's Wysart's." Kelly took a moment to appreciate Tamara's dress-for-success outfit: blazer, slim skirt, white shirt, low pumps. "You look subdued today."

Tamara jerked at the hem of her dark blue blazer. "It's my modern executive look." She leaned forward to place a hand on Kelly's arm. "Giving Julie the ax was tough, huh?"

"Not as bad as I'd thought it would be," Kelly admitted. "Julie made it easier by acting guilt-free."

Tamara sat back with a shrug. "Julie has a lot of maturing to get through. Her emotional growth stopped when she was ten."

Kelly kept from laughing by mentally admonishing herself for making light of someone else's misfortune. "Tamara, have you seen Beau Sullivan around here much?"

"Not at all," Tamara said, then held up one finger to amend her hastiness. "Hold on. I do remember seeing him a couple of nights ago, but he was on his way out of the department, I didn't know if he was passing through or if he'd been here for a while without me noticing." Tamara put on a worried expression. "It's not like me not to notice when a good-looker like him is nearby."

"He's the one who filed this report on Julie's indiscretions. He even interviewed one of her friends and got her to squeal on Julie." Kelly closed the folder and placed it in her employee file drawer, then locked it. "I was under the impression that he hadn't been anywhere near our department since Tuesday."

"Like I said, I haven't seen him except that one night. I think it was Thursday." Tamara made a tent with her fingers and looked across at Kelly with teasing eyes. "Has he been hanging around *you* much?"

"No." Kelly laughed and shook her head in a firm denial, ending that channel of discussion. "I wish he had let me know about Julie before he told Cauley."

"You mean he filed his report to Cauley before he mentioned it to you?"

"He has *yet* to mention it to me," Kelly amended. "I was thrown for a loop this morning when Cauley handed me this report. I had no idea that Julie was pulling these tricks."

"How long has she been giving her friends discounts?"

"Only during the last week or so, according to this report. Detective Sullivan did mention in his report that the department manager—he didn't drop names, but then he didn't have to—would have caught the discrepancy sooner or later. That was generous of him, don't you think?"

"Do I detect a fit of temper here?" Tamara asked with a wide-eyed gaze of wonder. "Can it be that Miss Happy-Go-Lucky is actually having a *bad* mood?"

"Oh, stop." Kelly laughed, mostly at herself for having gained the reputation of being constantly of good cheer. "I admit it. I'm human. Some people actually get on my nerves."

"Or under your skin," Tamara said.

"I'm going to forget you said that." Kelly pulled forward a stack of receipts. "Let's go over these before my shift ends," she said, abruptly steering the conversation from personal to professional.

Bette Zinquist propped her thonged feet up on the redwood railing. Her long legs were smooth and freckled but pale, since Bette avoided the sun. She was the type who never tanned; she burned.

"Well, what are you thinking?" Kelly persisted, having just told her best friend about her day of bad news and prickly agitation. "Am I being paranoid, or is Beau Sullivan picking on me?"

"I think," Bette said, squinting at the horizon where the sun was setting, spreading pink and violet across the sky. "No, I'm *wondering* why your life seems so much more exciting than mine."

"Bette," Kelly groaned, then propped her own feet on her patio railing. "My life isn't exciting."

"Not true. A handsome detective is solving crimes around you, and you think that's not exciting? Come to the alligator farm with me one day, and I'll show you dull. When you've seen one lumbering body, you've seen them all."

"You love those alligators," Kelly said.

"I love those alligators," Bette agreed, almost robot-like. "But I was referring to the guys I work with. I don't have a good-looking private detective hanging around, making my life interesting."

"You keep calling him good-looking, but you haven't seen him lately, so you're making a big assumption."

"I did see him." Bette looked at Kelly from the corner of her eye and smiled slyly. "I couldn't help myself the other night when I heard him pull into your driveway. I sneaked a peek out my front window." She waved a hand before her face and blew up to flutter her bangs. "He's a hot number, Kelly."

"He's my ex-brother-in-law."

"You keep repeating that as if it's important," Bette said with some irritation.

"It *is* important. He's Ryan's brother."

"Well, somebody's got to be. Don't blame poor Beau for something he can't help."

Kelly laughed and leaned sideways to poke Bette with her elbow. "Tell me what you think about Beau filing that report without letting me know about it first. Doesn't it sound as if he's trying to sabotage me?"

"Why would he?"

"I don't know. Maybe he didn't like it when I turned him down the other night."

"Turned him down about what?"

"He suggested that we start...well, dating. I told him to forget it."

THE SECOND MR. SULLIVAN 51

"And you think he's so emotionally arrested that he'd make you look bad at work just because you rejected him?"

"No, I guess not."

"Why don't you *ask* him why he didn't warn you about the trouble coming your way?"

"I was going to, but I haven't seen him around and I..." She thought about his kiss and her response. Her face and neck grew uncomfortably warm. "I don't want to encourage him. I didn't want him to think I was using it as an excuse to be around him."

Bette's feet hit the deck with a thump as she twisted around to stare at Kelly. "*He's* not emotionally arrested—*you* are! What went on between you two? I get the feeling that your dinner out with him created some kind of dilemma. Otherwise, why would you be afraid of crossed signals?"

"I'm not afraid."

"Then why not talk to him?"

"I just told you," Kelly insisted, squirming in the metal chair.

"Yes, you said you didn't want to encourage him, which is stupid."

"Bette, he—" Kelly chopped off her sentence as her mouth suddenly went dry with the memory of Beau's kisses.

"He what?"

"He kissed me," she blurted out with a rush of breath.

Bette's whole body slumped as if the air had been squeezed out of it. "Is that all? The way you're acting, I thought he'd demanded that you give him your firstborn son." She stood up and sat astride the railing, her long legs swinging. "What is it? That ex-brother-in-law stuff again?"

"Yes, and more than that." Kelly stared straight ahead at the heavy-headed sea oats lolling in the breeze. "Bette, I haven't felt like that in years and years."

Bette's laugh was not mocking, only compassionate. "And that feeling scared you silly."

"Yes!" Kelly placed her hand where her heart triphammered at the memory. "I'm thirty-two years old! Too old for that crazy, dazy, giddy, aw-shucks-ain't-love-grand feeling. I hate that stuff. I thought I was past it. I especially don't want to feel that way about *him*."

"Honey, do you know how many lonely people out there would give a month's salary to know what you're feeling?" Bette stared deeply into Kelly's moist eyes. "Don't be afraid of it, and don't get bent out of shape just because his last name is the same as yours. It's not fair to you or to him."

"It's not that simple," Kelly objected. "I know you can't always choose who you want to love, but you *can* choose who you want in your life, and I've had all the Sullivans I want."

The doorbell ended the round of debate. Kelly forced herself up from the chair and went through the darkened house to the front door. She pressed an eye to the peephole and couldn't believe that Beau Sullivan was actually standing on her front porch, all starchy white in cotton trousers and open-throated shirt. She glanced over her shoulder to find that Bette had stepped inside the house and was waiting for her to open the door to the caller.

"It's him," Kelly whispered.

Bette propped her hands at her waist in a stern pose. "Well, let him in, scaredy-cat!"

Kelly switched on a table lamp before she opened the door with reservation. She arched a brow inquisitively when Beau beamed at her.

"Hi, Kelly. I should have called, but—"

"Yes, you should have. I've got company."

"Do you?" He peered into the living room. "Oh, sorry. I guess I can come back later when—"

"Ask him in, Kelly," Bette said as she came forward into the lamp light. "You don't remember me, but we went to the same high school. I'm a few years older than you."

Beau stepped over the threshold to shake her hand. "Bette, isn't it?"

"Yes!" Bette gave him a firm handshake. "You actually remember me?"

"Sure. You were on the girls' basketball team."

"What a memory," Bette said, laughing. "I live next door. I just dropped in to gossip with my neighbor. Actually, we were just talking about you," Bette said, linking an arm through his and pulling him along toward the sliding patio door. She glanced over her shoulder long enough to glare playfully at Kelly.

"Should I apologize or be flattered?" Beau asked.

Bette laughed, but her voice remained as droll as ever. "Both. Kelly was telling me that you're a detective and that you stabbed her in the back today."

Kelly groaned softly and dropped into one of the bright yellow chairs. She stared daggers at her friend before lifting her gaze to the man standing beside her. His brows met in a scowl of concern as he shifted from one foot to the other.

"I was afraid you might think that," he said so softly that his voice was almost drowned out by the cry of a passing gull. "That's why I stopped by this evening on my way home. I wanted to clear my name."

"This should be interesting," Bette said with her deadpan delivery. "Wish I could stick around and hear it, but

I promised some of the guys at work that I'd join them in a poker game this evening."

"Where do you work?" Beau asked.

"At an alligator farm. It's about five miles up the highway."

"I've seen it. What do you do there?"

"Bette is the assistant supervisor," Kelly said with a hint of pride, knowing that Bette's position at the farm was more important than Bette would ever admit.

"I supervise the operation, not the gators. Gators, for the most part, do what they damn well please." She smiled at Beau's attractive laugh, then she turned her attention to Kelly's fretful expression. "I can go now, knowing that I'm leaving you in good hands." Bette's grin was full of female secrets. She bounded down the patio steps and went toward her own house.

The sun had set and dusk had become darkness. Kelly looked up at the starry night as Beau made himself comfortable in the chair beside her. His white clothes bewitched Kelly's peripheral vision, making her think of apparitions. Why was Beau haunting her? she wondered. And why had his kisses the other night spooked her so much? Bette was right. She was making too much of it. A kiss is just a kiss; a sigh is just a sigh.

"Why the long sigh?" Beau asked, startling her. "Is it a sign of boredom, or are you wishing I would vanish?"

"I wasn't even aware that I'd sighed," she confessed, pulling up from her slouched posture. "You stopped by for a reason?"

"I would have dropped by your office, but I wasn't at the mall today."

"Taking a day off?"

"No, I've been working on a different case." He studied his clasped hands for a moment before he went on.

"There are certain rules of conduct I have to follow, Kelly. I was hired by the mall executives, so that's to whom I must report my findings. I was sorely tempted to tell you about what I'd uncovered in your department, but that would have been unprofessional of me."

"That's how you see it?" she asked archly.

"Yes, and that's how *you'd* see it if you and I hadn't been out together a couple of times and if we hadn't shared a few intimacies along the way."

"I don't know what you're getting at."

"Simple. You wouldn't have expected me to confide in you about my investigations if I was only a professional acquaintance. No matter how much I wanted to tip you off, I couldn't. I did what I was hired to do. I reported the perpetrator to management, and they, in turn, contacted Joe Cauley."

Kelly heaved herself to her feet and waited for Beau to do the same. Then she grabbed his hand and shook it briskly, ignoring his rattled chuckle.

"Thanks for stopping by with that explanation. Let me see you to the door." She started to turn away from him, but he jerked her back to face him.

"Hold on." He gripped her upper arms, making her stand before him and listen. "Don't use that phony nonchalance with me. I'm being honest with you, and I expect the same in return."

She twisted free of him, backed off until she felt secure, and allowed her stinging feelings to surface in biting, trembling words. "I wish you'd pick on somebody else for a change. I mean, who asked you to clean up *my* department? Couldn't you have just as easily scouted housewares? How about ladies' wear? They could use a man around the place."

"I'm not picking on your department."

"Well, it sure looks that way to me. First the credit-card thief, and now you. It's a double play. One more, and I'm out."

"Is that what Cauley suggested to you? If so, he's crazy. You had nothing to do with it. Besides, given time, you would have discovered the discrepancies."

"Right, so why did you stick your nose into it?"

"Because that's what I'm hired to do," he answered, his voice lowering in pitch with his increased ire.

"You were hired to catch the credit-card thief, not to undermine me at every turn."

"Let me ask you something—and I want an honest answer."

Kelly lifted her chin to eye him with resentment. "Despite what you might think of me, I'm not a liar."

He acted as if he might respond to her implication, but then he shook his head as if it wasn't worth the trouble. "Are you mad at me about what's happening at work or about what's happening between us?"

She fixed an innocently, befuddled look on her face. "What's happening between us?"

"You know."

"No, I don't." She strolled past him, moving slowly toward the patio door. "All I know is that you seem to think you're God's gift to women, but I don't."

"Are you truly mad because I discovered a thief in your department? Think about it. Your anger is misdirected, Kelly."

"And you've worn out your welcome." She held out one arm, indicating the front door. "One Sullivan in my life was quite enough. Please leave."

"Kelly, let's talk about this. I like you. I don't want us to be enemies over something this petty."

She stood her ground, her face set in an unrelenting frown. Beau muttered an anathema under his breath and strode past her. The front door slammed behind him. Seconds later Kelly heard a car engine and the squeal of tires.

She expected to feel triumphant, but she felt small. She sat on the patio for more than an hour, sorting out her feelings and discarding one excuse after another. Was she being unfair to Beau? she worried. Could it be that she was trying to make him accountable for his brother's sins?

Juggling a briefcase, a Styrofoam cup of coffee and a sack containing two jelly doughnuts in one hand and searching for his office key with the other, Beau was almost upon Ryan before he noticed him.

"Whoa, brother," Ryan said, laughing as he reached out to grasp Beau's shoulders. "Some detective you are!"

"Good morning to you, too, Ry." Beau unlocked the door and pushed it open. "After you." He scowled at his brother's back before entering the office and closing the glass-paned door, with its brand-new lettering proclaiming that the office belonged to Sullivan Detective Agency.

Beau set his breakfast on the desk, then removed his lightweight suit coat and hung it on the coat tree in one corner of the small, sunlit office. Ryan strolled around the perimeter, hands tucked in the pockets of his trousers. He paused at the wall calendar, the bottled water dispenser and the framed certificates and licenses. Ryan was a good-looking man with strawberry-blond hair and a lightly freckled complexion. Beau recalled that a few years ago Ryan had been slightly overweight, but his second wife was an aerobics instructor, and she'd whipped him back into shape. Now he was health conscious and spent most of his free time jogging or swimming. He refused to eat meat, and sugar never touched his lips.

"If I'd known you were coming, I would have brought you some coffee, too," Beau said, sitting down in the wooden swivel chair.

"I don't drink that poison," Ryan said sanctimoniously. "You're going to lose customers if you don't keep regular office hours." Ryan finished his tour and sat in one of the other chairs.

"Ry, I'm a detective, not a shopkeeper." Beau removed the lid from the coffee and sniffed the steam curling from it. "I can't solve cases from inside this office."

"Hire a secretary to keep the office open," Ryan said with a shrug. He was crisply all business in his pinstriped suit, pale blue dress shirt, striped tie and highly polished shoes.

"I might do that someday." Beau sipped the coffee, then pulled one of the doughnuts from the white sack. "Did you come here to give me pointers, or do you have something else on your mind?"

Ryan examined the doughnut with obvious distaste. "You're going to kill yourself by eating that junk."

"We all gotta go sometime...somehow." Beau took a gigantic bite to irritate his younger brother. "So, what's your story?" he asked around the gooey concoction.

Ryan released his jacket button and slanted one ankle across the other knee. "I mainly wanted to see your office. How long are you planning on sticking around this time?"

"Your guess is as good as mine."

"In other words, this is temporary," Ryan said, spreading out his hands to encompass the room.

"Not exactly. I'm trying to establish an agency here, and if it works out, I'll stay. If it doesn't, I'll have to relocate."

"But you want to stay in this detecting business?"

"Sure. Why not?" Beau finished the first doughnut and reached for the second. He wadded the white sack into a neat ball, took careful aim, and tossed it toward the trash barrel several feet away. It dropped neatly inside. "Two points," Beau said, grinning.

"Ashley and I were over at the folks' last night," Ryan said, ignoring Beau's playfulness. "They said that you were working with Kelly."

Beau lounged back, relaxing now that the cat was out of the bag. He munched on the doughnut and slurped the coffee, knowing that Ryan mightily disapproved of every bite and every sip.

"How is she?" Ryan asked when it was apparent that Beau wasn't going to offer information.

"Busy. She's managing the men's department at Wysart."

"Yes, but... healthwise, how is she?"

"Healthwise?" Beau repeated with a chuckle. "To tell you the truth, Ry, I haven't gotten around to asking about her last checkup." He grinned at Ryan's sigh of irritation. "On the outside she looks fine."

"I know she took the divorce hard," Ryan explained.

"But that was almost three years ago. She survived." Beau popped the last of the doughnut into his mouth and washed it down with the tepid coffee. "She seems to be doing well for herself. She's got a house near the ocean."

"You've been to her house?"

"Yes," Beau revealed, studying his brother's face for any hint of disapproval.

"So, it's true. The folks said that you two were dating."

"Not exactly dating," Beau corrected. "It's not that structured. I took her to dinner. That's it."

"Would you like to see her again?" Ryan asked.

Beau hesitated before he answered. He was uncomfortable with the line of questioning, so he decided to make Ryan just as uncomfortable. "Did you *really* invite her to your wedding?"

Ryan's square chin edged up arrogantly. "Yes. What of it?"

"It amazes me, that's all," Beau said with a shrug. "I hope you didn't think she'd actually show up with wedding gift in hand."

"I was merely being polite. What else has Kelly told you?"

"Look, let's get something straight right off," Beau said, pushing up from the chair and tossing the Styrofoam cup into the trash. "I'm not going to *gossip* with you about Kelly. I have respect for you and her, so don't put me in the middle. If you've come here to get the lowdown on what she's—"

"You've got it all wrong," Ryan roared, jumping up from his chair to confront his taller brother. "That's *not* why I'm here."

"Then tell me why you *are* here," Beau insisted.

"To tell you I think it's great that you and Kelly are seeing each other!"

Beau angled backward an inch or two to study Ryan's face. Honesty radiated from it.

"Kelly is a wonderful woman, and she needs a good man. I'm glad she's dating you," Ryan explained.

Beau sat down again, but Ryan remained standing. "Thanks," he said shortly, still uncomfortable discussing Kelly with Ryan. "How's Ashley? I haven't seen her since I've been back."

"She's happy. We're happy." Ryan strolled to the arched window and examined the view.

"And how's the insurance business?"

"Great. Just great. In fact, I might be up for a promotion."

"No kidding? What kind of promotion?"

"It's too early to talk about it," Ryan said, turning from the window. "I've got to get back to work. Give Kelly my best regards when you see her again." He glanced around once more and nodded. "Yes, this isn't too bad."

"Gee, thanks," Beau said sarcastically. He stood up and shook his brother's hand. "Stop by anytime, Ry. Let me know ahead of time, and I'll stock up on bean sprouts."

"Go ahead and make fun," Ryan said, shaking a cautionary finger at Beau as he made his way to the door. "Someday you'll wish you'd listened to me."

"Yeah, that'll be the day." Beau laughed, dodging Ryan's shadow punch. "Take care of yourself and Ashley."

Beau went back to his desk, swung his feet up on it and laced his fingers behind his head. He went over the conversation he'd had with Ryan and read between the lines. Ryan had a guilty conscience, Beau surmised. Ryan must have dropped so much misery on Kelly that he was hoping some other man would right his wrongs. Even if that man happened to be his brother.

He laughed lightly at the twist of fate, and then his thoughts latched on to Kelly. His attraction to her was powerful, so much so that her tirade yesterday had left him unshaken in his resolve to involve himself in her life. If he had doubts, he had only to think of the few kisses they'd shared and any doubt disintegrated. Kelly was no passing fancy.

Could someone actually fall in love so quickly? He pondered the question but quickly realized there was no definitive answer. Love was a puzzle, solved differently by each set of players. But he was sure of one thing. To solve the puzzle, he needed a partner.

"You're not going to get rid of me so easily, Kelly Sullivan," Beau said aloud, his voice gruff with determination.

Four

The hammering drew her to the break room like a magnet draws metal shavings. Kelly stood transfixed in the doorway, her lower jaw dropping a fraction as she stared at the four men, who were installing rainbow-colored lockers against one wall. A minute later she noticed the fifth man, standing in the far corner and wearing a smile that could melt the coldest of hearts.

Beau came forward, dodging the workmen and clutter. He stopped and turned to extend an arm toward the workers.

"Ta-daaa," he trumpeted, then faced her again. "You're finally getting your lockers. Happy now?"

Kelly propped one shoulder against the door frame, shaking her head slowly at the ways of the world. "They hire me to run the department, make improvements where necessary, offer suggestions whenever possible, but they ignore my input. Then you come along and they leap to do your bidding." She laughed, but it was bitter. "Explain it all to me, Mr. Sullivan. You seem to have all the answers."

He laughed, but he wasn't amused. "I just can't please you, can I? I thought this might mend some fences between us. You wanted these lockers, so I used my leverage to get them installed today. I had foolishly hoped that you'd thank me instead of chopping me off at the knees." He seemed to be waiting for her to throw the next punch.

Kelly weighed his side of the argument and decided he had every right to be miffed at her reaction.

"I'm sorry," she said, wincing at the effort it took to say those two words. "I'm griping at you for something that isn't your fault. The lockers should put our thief out of business, don't you think?" she asked, looking on the brighter side.

"Hopefully, but I would like to catch him, instead of making him move to a different shopping center to ply his trade."

"How long will these men be here?" Kelly asked, moving away from the noise.

"They should be finished by late this afternoon," Beau said, falling into step beside her. "How about lunch today? We can go somewhere quiet and mend some more fences."

Kelly decided at that second that he was the most persistent man she'd ever met. "I brought my lunch," she said, smiling at the belief that she'd cut him off at the pass.

"I can grab something to go and meet you somewhere."

Kelly laughed at his tenaciousness. "I don't know when I'll be able to get away for lunch." She hoped her smile conveyed her "nice try" feeling toward him. "Some other time." She saw the store's visual manager and signaled to him. "Excuse me, but I've got to coordinate a new display." She didn't give him a chance to detain her as she all but shouldered him aside to speak with the display manager, who would assist her in creating an eye-catching array of shirts and ties for the upcoming September Surprises sale.

It was almost two o'clock by the time Kelly was finished with the displays. The din coming from the break room hadn't diminished, so she grabbed her purse and the sack containing her chicken sandwich, corn chips and clump of grapes and left the department store. She bought a soft drink and went to the center of the mall, where a bubbling fountain was surrounded by wide, smooth benches. Sunlight streamed down from a skylight, and midsize trees created the sense of oasis in a concrete desert. Kelly sat on one of the benches and withdrew the bag of chips and her wax paper-wrapped sandwich. She munched happily for a few minutes before sensing that she was being watched—no, stared at. She glanced over her shoulder. Beau Sullivan sat no more than a foot from her.

"You!" Kelly said, making the word a blatant accusation. "What are you doing here?"

He held up a box of popcorn and a soft drink. "Having lunch. Is there a law against it?"

"You're following me, when I made it clear that I didn't want to have lunch with you," she said, turning her back on him.

"Just pretend I'm not here," he suggested smoothly.

"No problem," she said, irritated with herself for smiling at his ploy. Persistent, she thought again. Stubborn and hardheaded, she added to the list. His arm brushed against her back, and she realized he had slid closer to her. She could feel his body heat, and it made her tingle all over.

"This is a great place to watch people," he said after a while. "Kelly...Kelly!" He grabbed her shoulder and jostled her.

"What?" she said, slightly irritated at being shaken. She edged away from him.

"See that woman?"

"Which woman?" she asked, looking about and responding to the sense of conspiracy in his voice. Did this have anything to do with the credit-card thief? she wondered, looking frantically for a suspicious-looking woman.

"That woman standing in front of the jewelry store. She's wearing a white blouse and a red jumper."

Kelly located the woman. She was in her thirties, reed thin, and carrying a toddler in her arms. Her hair was light brown, hanging straight to her shoulders, and she wore no visible makeup.

"Yes, I see her. What about her?" Kelly asked, unable to recognize the woman or determine Beau's objective.

"She's an adult film star who bares all for the silver screen," he whispered, so close that his breath stirred the fine hair at her temple. "The baby is her sister's. Usually she's mobbed in restaurants and shops, thus the kid as a kind of disguise. Nice touch, huh?"

Kelly twisted around to see his face. She strained back to get a better look at his dancing eyes and deepening dimples. "You're pulling my leg, right?"

He chuckled at her teasing, then scouted the milling crowd. "It's a game I play sometimes. I zero in on a person and guess what he or she does for a living. Of course, my imagination runs to the more colorful occupations. Take that man over there." He nodded in the general direction. "The one in the flowered shirt and red shorts. Got him in your cross hairs yet?"

"Got him," Kelly said, fixing her gaze on the paunchy man in his forties, who carried a sack from a discount clothiers. She didn't pull away when Beau's shoulder pressed against hers.

"He's one of our country's most famous fashion designers," Beau said, almost comical in his sincerity.

"No!" Kelly scoffed, joining in with his game.

"On my honor," Beau assured her, placing one hand over his heart. "He's wearing that atrocious outfit simply to conceal his identity."

"The shopping bag is a nice diversion," Kelly noted, then spotted her own target. "Hey, isn't that... Yes, it is!"

"What? Who?" Beau asked, his gaze darting frantically.

"The young boy standing outside the video rental store. He's ten or eleven, wearing blue jeans and a green T-shirt."

"Right, I see him."

She leaned sideways, speaking from one corner of her mouth. "Computer whiz," she confided. "He deals in obtaining Soviet secrets and Middle East oil strategies."

"Who would have guessed?" Beau shook his head, amazed. "A kid like that." He turned sideways toward her. "Do you think anyone could guess that we're locked in a battle of wills?"

"We are?"

"Sure." He lowered his head a fraction to lock gazes with her. "Will she give him another chance, or will she continue to make him grovel at her feet?"

Kelly felt color fan up from her neck into her face. She began stuffing litter into the paper sack. "I can't imagine you groveling at anyone's feet, Beau. I'm not trying to make you pay for anything. I just don't think it's wise for us to see each other."

"You said that it was okay for us to be friends."

"I still think it's okay, but seeing each other socially complicates things. You said so yourself. The thing with Julie Scott and the lockers today—it all would be easier to take if I didn't feel a personal connection to you."

"If you already feel it, why fight it?"

"Because..." She paused, knowing that she couldn't tell him the unvarnished truth, because it eluded even her. "Because I'm not that attracted to you," she said, then looked up at him through her lashes. His gentle smile told her that he didn't buy her explanation for one second.

"Why don't you have dinner with me tonight and we'll thrash this out to our mutual satisfaction?"

"No." She stood and placed one hand on his shoulder to keep him seated. "I've got to get back to work. Beau, be a friend and leave this as it is." She smiled but knew it wasn't convincing. "I think it will be better for us all the way around." She discarded her paper sack in a trash dispenser and walked swiftly away before Beau could shoot down her vague reasoning.

The ominous *click, click* sent a wave of frustration through Kelly. She pounded the steering wheel with her fist and growled furiously at the car.

"I can't believe this! You lousy bucket of bolts." She tried the ignition again and listened to the metallic tick of failure. A shadow passed over the other shadows in the underground parking lot, and Kelly looked around nervously. She heard footsteps directly behind her. She twisted in the seat, slamming home the door lock as she did. The side mirror revealed a glimpse of red hair and a smirky grin. Beau Sullivan leaned over a little so that she could get a good look at his smug expression. Kelly slumped forward, draped her arms on the steering wheel and rested her forehead on them.

"I should have known it was you," she said after giving her heart a few moments to slow its pace. She rolled down the window and fell back against the car seat. "Johnny-on-the-spot Sullivan."

"Having trouble, ma'am?"

"Nothing but." She motioned to the hood. "It's all yours. As usual, I'm at your mercy."

"If only that were true," he said, moving to the front of the car to lift the hood.

"Got your pocketknife?" Kelly asked.

"I don't think that will help this time."

"Why? Did someone steal my engine?"

"No." He closed the hood and took out his handkerchief. He wiped streaks of grime from his hands as he came to the driver's window. "I think your battery is too weak to turn her over this time."

"Do you have jumper cables?"

"No, not with me. Tell you what. I'll drive you home, take you to work tomorrow and check out your car. I can probably get it going and save you a bundle of money. How about it? Will you let me help you out, or are you going to cut off your nose to spite your face?"

She lifted one hand and felt her nose, making him chuckle. Tiny lines fanned from his expressive, sparkling eyes. In that moment Kelly thought he was the most attractive man she'd ever known. "Think I'll keep it."

"I don't blame you," he said, opening the door and helping her out of her car. "It's adorable."

Kelly shot him a warning glance. "Cut that out, buster. I'm accepting your offer to help, but that doesn't mean I've changed my mind. I have enough complications in my life," she said, sighing heavily and then slamming the car door as she made a hateful face at her traitorous car. "I don't need any more, thank you very much."

His sleek sports car was parked a dozen cars away. Kelly let him open the door for her, then shut it after she'd settled into the comfortable leather seat. Through half-closed eyes, she watched him walk around to the other side. His jeans looked new, dark blue with gold stitching. He wore a blue-plaid shirt of varying shades, a navy tie and suit jacket. He climbed in beside her, and Kelly glanced down at his rubber-soled deck shoes and dark socks. Not bad, she thought, closing her eyes as he started the car and reversed from the parking space. She could make a marginal improvement by selecting a tie of a lighter color and a less nondescript jacket. However, his clothes fit well and had obviously been chosen with comfort in mind.

"Tiring day?" he asked, and Kelly knew that he'd been glancing her way, because she could sense his keen regard.

"Yes, and my car trouble didn't help matters."

"Don't worry about that. I'm sure I'll be able to fix it. Won't cost you a dime."

"If you buy parts, I want to pay for them," she said, lifting her head and opening her eyes. He nodded congenially, but she wasn't sure he was in total agreement with her instructions. "I mean it, Beau."

"I hear you, Kelly," he said, smiling faintly. "Your voice carries."

She settled back again, eyes closed. Minutes later, when the car began to slow down, she sat up and looked around, startled.

"What's going on? Why are we stopping?" she asked. Beau was beginning to turn the car off the road and into some sort of resort. "Are you low on gas or something?"

"This is where I live," he said, sending the car past a sentry post and onto a tree-lined street. "I thought we'd stop at my place for dinner before I take you home."

"Oh, you did, did you?" she asked, her voice rising noticeably as she shifted in the seat to face him. "Beau, I am *not* amused."

"Kelly, I am *not* trying to amuse you. I'm only being nice, courteous, a good friend to one in need." He parked the car in front of a long motor home. "Every Irishman has to have a castle. Mine has wheels. Six, to be exact. What do you think?" he asked, turning his smile on her.

"I think that I'm too tired to argue with you. I'll eat, and then you *will* take me straight home."

"I will. Promise." He reached across her to open the door, laughing under his breath when she jumped all over at his sudden movement. "Take it easy, Kelly. I'm practically harmless."

"It's the 'practically' that's got me worried." She got out of the car and examined Beau's castle.

It was white, with a red, blue and gold band running horizontally all the way around it. The big, tinted windows were evenly spaced, and a blue and gray awning on one side shielded a patio area. Beau had spread a square of artificial turf under the awning, and the two chairs, lounger and grill looked inviting. The RV park had provided a concrete picnic table and benches.

"Good evening, Beau," a woman called from the trailer next to his.

"Hello, Evelyn. Did you and Jim have any luck yesterday?"

"Not bad. We caught a few snapper and grouper. If we catch some this evening, I'll bring a mess over to you."

"Thanks," Beau said, patting his stomach. "I can always put away a few fish. You know that."

Kelly walked with Beau to the door. He unlocked it, and when he opened the door, two electronic steps slid into place.

"Go on inside," he urged, cupping her elbow in one hand while he flung open the screen door with the other. "It's a thirty-two footer, so there's plenty of room."

To her surprise, she discovered that he was right. Finding herself in a living room that contained a plush sofa and matching rocker, Kelly looked toward the back at a kitchen, dining area, bedroom and bath. At the front, the driver's and passenger chairs had been swiveled around to provide two extra seats for the living room. Full drapes ran around the front windshield, providing privacy and making one forget that this home had a dashboard, brake and accelerator.

A color television sat on the lower shelf of a corner cabinet, and a basket of silk flowers and a short stack of novels took up the top shelf. Kelly moved closer to examine the books' spines. They were all current best-sellers, running in the mystery and suspense vein.

"You like?" Beau asked, stepping around her to the kitchen.

"Yes, it's really nice. I love this color scheme. Peach and aqua are favorites of mine."

"Have you been inside one of these before?"

"No. I had no idea they could be so... so homey." She tried out the rocker and found it to be sturdy and comfortable. "How long have you lived on wheels?"

"Let's see..." He did some mental calculations while he removed his jacket and hung it in a closet just inside the bedroom. "Almost four years now. This is my second motor home. I bought it a little over a year ago. My other one was a few feet shorter than this." He removed his tie and freed the top two shirt buttons, then secured an apron around his lean waist. The apron had apples and oranges needlepointed on it. "A present from my mom," he explained, touching one of the apples. "She's handy with a needle, if you remember."

"Yes, I remember." She swiveled her chair around so that he couldn't see the uneasiness she knew was reflected in her face. His comment brought home once more their previous connection. Kelly cleared her throat nervously. "Do you like living like this?"

"Like what?"

"Well, you know, like a gypsy. Don't you ever want to have a home that doesn't move unless there's an earthquake?"

"I used to have an apartment, but my work kept me on the road and I spent most of my time in hotels." He opened the refrigerator and pulled out a couple of root beers. He opened the bottles and handed one to her. "I'd offer you a real beer, but I don't have any at the moment."

"I like these better," Kelly said, then took a drink. It was icy cold. "*Much* better," she added. "What work were you doing that kept you hopping around?"

"That's when I was working for the Bureau, then later I got into insurance adjusting and investigation of claims for a region that included four states." As he talked, he began mixing a pizza dough from scratch. "I decided I might as well give up my apartment and get one of these so I could at least cook my own meals and sleep in my own bed most of the time. The RV parks around the country are clean and quiet, and the people are so friendly that it makes traveling a pleasure instead of a pain. Even if I buy a house someday, I still want to keep a motor home for vacations. It's the only way to travel."

"And you've already made friends here," she said, looking out the window to the trailer next door.

He glanced out the kitchen window. "It's easy to make friends here. On the other side is a retired couple. They're snowbirds."

"They're what?"

"Snowbirds," he repeated. "People who live in warm climates during the winter and then head north in the spring."

"Oh, I see." She studied his cooking preparations with concern. "Beau, frozen pizza would be fine with me. You don't have to go to such trouble."

"Frozen pizza?" He made a face as if he'd bitten into a lemon. "I'd just as soon spread some tomato sauce over a piece of cardboard. This is no trouble, really. It'll be ready in a jiffy. I hope you like Canadian bacon and lots of cheese."

"My favorite," she admitted, earning a brilliant smile from him.

Something caught his eye outside the window, and he washed the flour from his hands and dried them on his apron as he went to the front door.

"Excuse me just a minute," he said to Kelly before he opened the door to the freckle-faced boy outside, whose arms were full of a wriggling, red dachshund. "Hey, Timmy, how did Foot Long fare today?"

"Came in second, right behind Mrs. Oxbow's terrier."

"Second place!" Beau took the dog from the boy, then waved aside the ribbon the youngster offered him. "No, you keep that," he said, then withdrew a dollar bill from his pocket. "And take this. Go on, take it. You earned it."

"Thanks, Mr. Sullivan. Want me to come around Saturday and help you wash your car?"

"I'll let you know tomorrow, Timmy. I've got company right now."

"Oh, okay. See you later."

"Later, my man." Beau closed the door and set the squirming dog on all fours. "Kelly meet Foot Long. Foot Long, Kelly."

"He...I mean, she's adorable," Kelly said, leaning over to stroke the dog's smooth head. "What did she win second in?"

"The RV park sponsored a pet show today. Timmy doesn't have a pet, so I let him borrow mine. Timmy's a good kid. He lives with his mother a couple of rows over. She works in the park's grocery store." Beau slid his finished pizza into the oven, then sat on the sofa. Foot Long jumped up beside him and stretched out, oblivious to the stranger across from her.

"She seems well adjusted," Kelly observed.

"She's been through it all." He rubbed the animal between her floppy ears. "I found her wandering in the desert outside Las Vegas. She was about a year old, thirsty and frightened. I adopted her, but it took a good six months before she got over her trauma and put it all behind her."

"How old is she now?"

"The vet says she's about four, maybe five. She's a good traveler, and she loves kids. She barks her head off if she hears a noise, but I've never known her to bite anyone. She's one smart wiener dog."

Seeing him sitting there in an apron, petting his faithful dog and enjoying his cozy home, Kelly laughed softly. "I'm sorry," she apologized, "but this is not the way I ever pictured you." She rested her head against the back cushion and propped her root-beer bottle against the knee of her black slacks. "I always thought that you were staying in exotic places. Hotel rooms with a view of the sea, beach bungalows, penthouses overlooking sparkling cities." She rotated her free hand in the flicking wave of the rich and famous. "I saw you with an ever-changing companion. Blondes, brunettes, redheads, and some in between. I *never* pictured you living in a comfortable motor home with an affectionate dog at your side." She lifted the wet bottle, revealing a damp ring on the knee of her slacks.

"Let me get you a coaster," he said, rising up from the sofa to fetch a cork-lined rectangle, which he set on the corner table. "I wasn't always like this," he said after he'd sat on the sofa again. "I used to enjoy the kind of life you described, but the past few years have been different. I've slowed down the pace. I'm taking time to enjoy the little things in life."

"Personally, I think that what you had before sounds pretty good." She sat the damp bottle on the coaster. The aroma of the pizza floated from the oven, stirring up her taste buds and making her stomach rumble. "Did you go to college?"

"Yes, I majored in police science."

"I wish I'd gone to college instead of getting married right out of high school," she said, drifting into a melancholy mood. "My parents tried to talk me into waiting a couple of years before I married Ryan, but I wouldn't listen. Being out on my own scared me. My parents had sheltered me, and I didn't want to be alone. That's what college meant to me. Being alone in a strange place around a bunch of strange people. I was so repressed back then."

"But take a look at you now," he said softly.

Kelly raised her head, drawn by the purring quality of his voice, which sent a current of excitement through her. His eyes were leaf green in the subdued light. He reached out one hand across the space between them and waited for her to respond. She hesitated only a few moments before placing her hand in his. He clasped it, squeezing without hurting, speaking without talking, then he stood up and let go of her to check on the pizza.

What had just happened? Kelly wondered. Nothing, really. Palm against palm. Eyes seeking eyes. But then something important had transpired. Something almost mystical. He had sought a reaction, and she had given it. But for the life of her, she didn't know precisely what she'd given, only that it had taken her one step closer to him.

"Pizza is ready," he said, placing the spicy disc on the dinette table. "Come and get it. Want another root beer?"

"No, I've still got some." She brought the bottle with her to the dinette. "Oh, Beau, this looks delicious," she said, sliding into the seat and sniffing at the steam rising up from the pizza.

Beau set the table, then sliced the pizza into wedges. He served Kelly, then himself, and sat opposite her. Kelly was in dining heaven from the first bite. She rolled her eyes and moaned. Beau laughed but didn't try to make conversation, as if sensing that she would rather attack the food than make polite chatter.

When only three pieces remained, Kelly sat back and shook her head when Beau started to serve her one of them.

"You're not quitting, are you?" he asked.

"Yes! I'm stuffed. Oh, but it was so good."

"Aren't you glad your car didn't start?"

"Well..." She laughed at herself. "Yes, I am glad. I would have thrown together a salad and missed out on the best pizza I've ever tasted. Really, you should go into the pizza business."

"I'll keep that in mind, in case my current business goes belly-up."

"How are things going for you?" Kelly asked as Beau cleared the table, placing what few dishes there were into the dishwasher.

"Pretty good. I've got two or three cases. Once I've cracked them, then word of mouth should start spreading. I'm hoping to eventually branch out into the security business, but I want to gain a reputation for myself before I do that." He removed the apron and hung it on a peg. "How about a cup of coffee?"

"No, thanks." Kelly roused herself from her lethargy, which was created by a hard day at work, a satisfying meal and good company. "Beau, I really must go home. I'm beat."

"Okay." He'd rolled up his sleeves earlier, but now he flicked them down and buttoned the cuffs. "If I can't tempt you with a cup of coffee or... ice cream?"

"No." She laughed as she slid to her feet and retrieved her purse from the living-room table.

"Then I guess I have no alternative than to take you straight home."

"Thank you," she said, sighing the word for effect, but she was serious when she added, "Beau, you're good company and a gracious host."

"Then you'll want to do this again soon?" He opened the front door for her after signaling Foot Long to stay put.

Kelly decided the prudent thing to do was not to answer him. She got into his sports car, feeling her resolve weaken with each smile he gave her and every kindness he bestowed upon her. A few days ago she'd agreed to a friendship with him, but his kisses and other advances had made her realize that a casual friendship might be out of the question. He had been doggedly persistent all day, getting his way at every turn. She wondered if she had the strength or the heart to keep up her end of the tug-of-war. What had been her original purpose in all of this? It took her a few moments before she could remember, and that time-lapse alarmed her.

He's Ryan's brother, she reminded herself firmly as she stared straight ahead and barely acknowledged the idle chatter coming from Beau. You'd be a fool to get all wrapped up in Ryan's brother. What would the other Sullivans think? What would her own parents think? Maybe she should call them this evening and find out. She'd spoken to her parents only a few nights ago but had been careful not to mention Beau. What's one more long-distance call to Orlando, especially when she needed older and wiser advice.

"Earth to Kelly. Earth to Kelly. The Eagle has landed," Beau intoned next to her.

"What?" Kelly looked around. The car was parked in her driveway. "Oh, my. I was daydreaming, I guess." She got out of the car before Beau could get around to her side. "Beau, you don't have to walk me to the door. Beau, really, I can manage," she said, moving quickly to her house, but Beau never broke stride. "Don't bother. Beau!"

He mounted the steps to stand before her on the porch. "Yes?"

She laughed lightly and threw him a baffled glare. "Thank heavens! I thought you'd lost your hearing there for a moment. I suppose you were just ignoring me again."

"Kelly, there's no way on God's green earth that I could ignore you."

She had no time to construct a defense. His arms came around her waist in a flash of contact. Kelly was brought up flush against him, and then his mouth was on hers. She made a sound of protest in her throat, but it sounded feeble even to her ears. Her arms were around his neck before she was aware that she'd automatically put them there. But from that point on, automation had nothing to do with it.

Kelly strained closer to him, slanting her mouth across his and squeezing her eyes shut to eliminate everything but the burning pressure of his mouth. He parted his lips only a fraction so the tip of his tongue could trace the seam of her mouth. She kept her lips closed to tease him, but she allowed her hands to float up until her fingers slid through his silky hair. She curled her fingers, taking strands of his hair between them and scraping her nails on his scalp. He trembled, and his lips opened more; his tongue tapped impatiently against her shielding lips. Desire flared within her like a Roman candle, but a part of her cringed from the bright, hot light of it. Once burned, twice shy, chanted a voice somewhere deep in her subconscious.

Kelly groped for Beau's upper arms. Muscles bulged under her palms, making her acutely aware of his superior strength, but she pushed him from her with her own brand of feminine power.

"Beau, that's enough." She pushed his hands away from her waist and turned toward the door. Even though her hands trembled, she managed to unlock it without wasted seconds.

"Kelly, why are you so upset?"

She stepped over the threshold and only then faced him. "I'm not upset. I'm tired."

"Tired of me?"

She started to agree but couldn't. She shook her head, closing the door slowly. "Just tired."

When she was sure that he'd driven away, Kelly turned on the living-room lamp and sat in her favorite chair. She tried to reach her parents, but they weren't home. Their phone rang twenty times before Kelly gave up.

"I'm a mass of contradictions," she said, telling the empty room what she'd wanted to tell her mom and dad. "I think I know what's good for me, but I can't seem to act on it. I know what I should do, but I can't do it! Like tonight, I should have stopped that kiss before it even started, but I participated in it!" She groaned and held her hot face in her hands. "I like him so much. Why does he have to be Ryan's brother? It's not fair. It's just not fair!"

For a few minutes she let herself imagine being with Beau. If that happened, she'd eventually see his family again. She could easily imagine their uneasiness and hers. And what about seeing Ryan again? No matter that he was remarried. Once upon a time Ryan Sullivan had been the sun she had revolved around. The awkwardness, the censure, the speculation, she'd have to endure whirled inside her to create a funnel of intense foreboding.

"Can't happen," she said, rolling her head from side to side in a fretful denial. "Beau's the most wonderful man I've met in a long time, but he comes with too many strings attached. I've got to make him understand that. I've just got to!" She felt her lips tremble as a sob clawed at her throat. "While I'm still able," she added, knowing her weaknesses were beginning to far outweigh her strengths where Beau Sullivan was concerned.

Five

Beau's black Corvette was parked beside Kelly's the next evening when Kelly left Wysart. Beau was sitting in his purring car, but he got out as she approached.

"Did you fix mine?" Kelly asked, hoping he had.

"All fixed."

"Thank you," she said with heartfelt gratitude. "Was it anything serious?"

"No. It only took a few minutes to fix."

"Oh, good. You didn't have to wait around for me."

"No problem. I've only been waiting five or ten minutes." He opened the car door for her and made a sweeping, gentlemanly gesture. "Your carriage, ma'am."

"I really do appreciate all your help, Beau." Kelly noticed a curious, pinched look around his eyes and wondered if his day had been as worrisome as hers. "I guess you heard about Tamara."

He nodded. "The latest victim of the credit-card thief. That's *all* I've heard about today, believe me. I've spent most of the day here at the mall. You're the only one in your department now who hasn't been a victim."

"So, I'm next. Is that it?" she asked, getting into the car.

"If there's a pattern, yes, but I don't see one. The lockers should end the problem in your department. I'm pushing to have them installed in all the mall stores for employees, but I'm meeting resistance."

"That shouldn't bother you," Kelly said, closing the door, then starting the engine. "You're not only bullheaded; you're a top-notch mechanic. Sure I can't pay you something for your trouble?"

"No, I won't hear of it." He squatted beside the car, crossing his arms on the window ledge. "Cauley didn't give you grief over this last incident, did he?"

"No, but he's not pleased. I get the feeling he thinks I'm not keeping an eye on my department."

"It's not just your department that's getting hit," Beau reminded her. "Nearly every major outlet in the mall has had trouble."

"Yes, I know." Kelly listened to the rumble of the motor and smiled. "Thanks again, Beau. It was sweet of you to fix my car."

"It's the least I could do."

"Why do you say that? You aren't under any obligation to help me."

He stood up and grinned crookedly. "Your battery cables were loose. I tightened them."

She looked at him from the corner of her eyes and sensed that something was rotten in Denmark. "Couldn't you have done that yesterday?" she asked as calmly as she could manage.

"Sure." He shrugged, backing up as he added, "But if I'd done that, then you would have missed out on the best pizza you ever had, and *I* would have missed out on the best good-night kiss *I* ever had."

"In other words, you tricked me," Kelly said, needing no other answer than his off-center smirk. Her hands closed around the steering wheel until her knuckles showed white. Just when she was beginning to think he was giving her some space, not pushing to get his way, not trying to mold her to his image, he had to blow it! She didn't know if her anger stemmed from a sense of outrage or profound disappointment. She knew only that she was steaming mad. She jerked the car into gear.

"That's the last dirty trick you'll play on me, because I have no intention of having anything else to do with you," she flung at him, speaking only loud enough to be heard above the engine. "You disappoint me, Beau. I thought you had more class."

Then she sped away, ruining Beau's flustered attempt at an apology.

The night was deep purple and wind-tossed. Kelly made her way down to the beach, walking off the day's disappointments. When she reached the beach she stopped to roll the legs of her jeans up to just below her knees and to remove her sandals. Swinging her shoes by their straps, she walked on the shifting sand, avoiding pieces of shells and bits of seaweed. The moon lit a path for her. A strong air current stirred the clouds above her. It combed her hair back from her face and cooled her brow. Kelly buttoned her tangerine sweater, loving the nip in the air and the sting of sea spray on her face but shivering as the breeze grew damper, stronger. There was only one other person in sight, a fisherman a good half mile down the beach from her. He cast out, the line feeding from the long pole and dropping silently, sinuously into the inky ocean.

Kelly paused to examine a shell. It was a small pink conch that hadn't been broken up too badly during its journey from the ocean floor to the beach. She put it in her sweater pocket, then walked on with her head bent and her thoughts revolving slowly around Beau Sullivan. She was spending far too much time thinking about him, she knew, but she couldn't stop the merry-go-round in her head.

When she'd reached home and had given herself time to think about her burning anger at him, she realized that she was bitterly disappointed that he'd resorted to trickery to get his way with her. She wanted to trust Beau. She hadn't trusted a man since her marriage. In Beau she'd thought she'd found sincerity and honor. It was such a childish prank for him to pull! She kicked at the sand and sent up a shower of grit. Okay, so she hadn't made it easy for him lately, but that was no excuse for him to manipulate her into a date. Why couldn't he accept what she offered—a lovely friendship—and leave it at that? Did he have to corner her at every turn and test her will? So she responded to his kisses. That didn't mean she encouraged them.

She fumed when she recalled the words of gratitude she'd poured on him, when all the while he was undeserving and knew it! The weasel. Standing there with that lopsided grin and those devilish green eyes while she basted him with one sweet coating after another of thank-yous and you-really-shouldn't-haves.

When she drew near enough to the fisherman to nod a silent greeting, she turned around and started back the way she'd come. Up ahead another walker was coming her way. Someone else is walking off worries, Kelly mused, wrestling with her own.

She'd told Bette about Beau's trick, and Bette had found it amusing, even flattering! Kelly stopped and faced the ocean. Was she taking all this too seriously, too personally? It was her nature to look at life with a healthy sense of humor. She'd learned to roll with the punches. She knew that laughter healed wounds. Maybe she should have laughed with Beau, instead of getting so mad she felt as if she could spit nails. By flying off the handle, she'd sent him the wrong signals, making him believe that she cared so much about him that he could wound her deeply. Of course, she *did* care for him more than she wanted to, but he shouldn't know that. Her feelings for him were already too complicated. Yes, she should have laughed in his face and told him to go fly a kite. But even now she couldn't manage a smile or a chuckle. He'd tricked her. It hurt. Those are the facts, she thought, appalled at herself when tears stung the corners of her eyes. She started walking in the direction of her house again, letting the cold wind dry her tears.

The other walker was much closer now. A man in white shorts and a dark T-shirt, Kelly noted, looking down again at the scattered seashells. But then an image sizzled through her mind and her head snapped up. Kelly stopped, staring at the man coming toward her. She couldn't make out his face, but she knew his distinctive long-legged stride and the slight swagger of his shoulders. Beau Sullivan! Couldn't he leave her alone for more than a few hours at a time? Kelly spun around. The fisherman was gathering in his line, giving up his quest on this night. The beach stretched to vast infinity, but Kelly felt trapped, cornered, held by an invisible noose.

"Kelly! Kelly, please, wait there!"

Beau's voice carried to her, and Kelly held her breath. His voice was compelling in its urgency. For some strange reason, she wanted to hear what he had to say. She wanted to know how he was feeling on this restless, troubled night. Then his hands covered her upper arms, forcing her around to him, and she released her pent-up breath in a sigh of defeat. He looked the way she felt, bone tired, as if he'd been run ragged. His clothes were wrinkled, his hair windblown, his eyes narrowed and lacking their usual dancing pinpoints of light. He set his mouth in a grim line as he examined her resigned expression.

"What are you doing here?" she asked, her voice leaden, spiritless.

"Looking for you." He groaned, rolling his eyes in a sweep of self-ridicule. "I'm a louse. I know it. I shouldn't have tricked you, but I wanted to be with you, and you're so damned stubborn!" He slid his hands down her arms to grasp her wrists. "You had a good time at my place, didn't you? What was so terrible about it?"

"Beau, does Ryan know you're seeing me?"

He released a short, incredulous laugh. "Is that what this is all about? You're afraid of what Ryan might think?"

"I'm not, nor have I ever been, *afraid* of Ryan. Have you discussed me with Ryan?"

"Not really."

"What's that mean? A yes or no will suffice."

"Yes."

"You see how complicated things are for us?" she asked, shaking loose his hands. "Can't you understand that I don't want Ryan's nose in my business anymore? I'm through with him. I'm through with that stage of my life. It's been over for a long time, as far as I'm concerned, and I want to keep it that way."

"Ryan and I haven't talked much about you. Only that I'm working on a case that involves you. I didn't initiate the conversation. He did. He wanted to let me know that if I did start seeing you, he was all for it."

She laughed at that, thinking that Ryan had a lot of nerve. "Oh, really? That's a load off my mind," she said with stinging sarcasm.

"Look, I'm in your corner. Ryan has nothing to do with us."

"Just leave me alone, Beau. You're a nice guy, but I just wish you'd take a walk... without me. You want to make me happy? Go away."

"That's garbage, and you know it," he said, his voice low and tinged with anger. He landed a hand on her shoulder when she started to push past him. "Listen to me, Kelly. I apologize for lying to you about your car, but don't lie to yourself. I'm more to you than just a nice guy."

"Yes, you're Ryan's brother!"

"So what? You said it yourself. Your marriage to Ryan is history, so why not forget it?"

"I have!"

"Then why do you keep bringing Ryan into this?"

"You're not so thickheaded that you can't understand how uneasy I am around you." She pushed his hand off her shoulder, needing her own space without his contact. "I'm not comfortable when I'm with you. I don't enjoy myself when you're around."

He stared at her, brows lowered, hands riding his waist as he silently challenged her last statement until Kelly flung out her arms in a painful recantation.

"All right, so I *was* comfortable last night. I had a good time," she confessed.

"You kissed me back last night."

"Y-yes. I did." She turned aside to gaze at the whitecaps. "And after you left, I thought about what would happen if I kept seeing you. Beau, it wouldn't work for us. It's not natural."

"I'm Ryan's brother, not yours."

She looked over her shoulder at him, smiling faintly at his gentle jesting. The breeze combed through his hair, ruffling it into loose, short waves of deep russet.

"What would your parents think?" she asked, trying to make him see how complicated things would be for them.

He shrugged broadly, rudely. "Who gives a damn? Kelly, I stopped worrying about what my parents would think about my dates a long time ago."

"But you love them. You wouldn't want to upset them."

"Why would they be upset? They like you."

"Yes, but I was Ryan's wife. It...it's awkward. Don't you see?"

"No, I don't. What I *do* see is that you spend too much time worrying about what other people might think. You should live your own life, Kelly, and stop letting others make rules for you to follow." He took her gasp of outrage for that of shock. "That's right. Don't push me away just because you're afraid of what Ryan or my parents or your parents might think!"

"I'm not," she said, spinning around to him. He looked so smug, so sure of her motives, her inner workings, when he obviously didn't know a blessed thing about her! "I'm pushing you away because you're an arrogant, obnoxious, manipulating brute!" She stiff-armed him, shoving him back a step. His jaw dropped open in shock. "I'm not anybody's puppet, Beau Sullivan. Not Ryan's. Not yours. It's taken me a long time and a lot of pain, but I can finally say that I stand on my own two feet and I make my own way in this world, so don't you *dare* accuse me of obeying somebody else's rules!"

"Whew!" He stared at her with wide eyes. He held up his hands, palms toward her as if he were fending off further attack. "Did I touch a sensitive nerve or what?"

"You're darned right you did," she said, still fuming. "I was a scared little rabbit three years ago, but not anymore. I've learned something you've always taken for granted—you can't depend on anyone but yourself. If you do, then you're a fool and in for a big fall. I fell, but I'm standing tall now, so don't preach to me about independence. I've *earned* mine, pal." She poked a finger at the center of his chest, then marched away.

"Kelly... Kelly, wait up." Beau trotted toward her, catching her hand and swinging her around. She snatched her hand from his, and he grinned. "Now that you've straightened me out, how about if you have me over for dinner Friday night?"

"How about if I *what*?" she asked, flabbergasted by his one-track mind.

"I had you over—now it's your turn. Friday night's okay with me. How's it with you?"

Her first reaction was to scream, but his utter audacity made her laugh at him, herself, the whole fiasco.

"Well? What time do you want me here Friday?"

"Beau, you're a piece of work," she said, still laughing under her breath at his quicksilver moods. She started for her house again with Beau shadowing her every step. "Dinner here Friday? I don't think—"

He stepped in front of her, hands gripping her upper arms, eyes glinting with intensity. "Don't tell me what you think. Tell me what you *want*."

All the negatives melted under the heat of his gaze. Kelly examined her deepest yearnings and discovered a simmering desire, a divine attraction that transcended the friendship she'd been trying to cultivate. "I want..."

"Yes?" he asked, breathless, expectant.

She shook her head, slinging her thoughts into order. "I don't want to cook for you," she said, not caring that her snappy comeback disappointed him.

He shrugged in a resigned fashion. "I'll accept that for now. I'll cook."

"No!" She reached out to detain him, but he flung off her hand. "Beau, that's not what I had in mind."

"Seven o'clock Friday," he said, then turned and sprinted up the sloping sand to solid ground.

"Beau!" Kelly called uselessly, then punched the air in a burst of frustration. "Oh, rats!" She dropped to the sand and glared menacingly at the moon. Gradually, her self-directed anger subsided as the moon slipped lower in the purple sky. Her tragedy began to seem more like a comedy. It was a clash of wills, a battle of wits, but nothing to get so upset about!

"Oh, well," she said, sighing the words. She stood up and started for home. "At least I don't have to cook for him, so he's not getting *everything* his way."

Walking slowly through the men's department, Kelly checked the copy of a sales advertisement with the merchandise situated near the aisles. She'd given Tamara the responsibility of arranging the sales items for the campaign that would begin in the morning. Kelly remembered the first time she'd been given this task and how she'd moved one rack of shirts to a dozen different locations until she'd finally found an eye-catching spot at the end of one aisle. She'd been given high marks by her sales manager with points taken off only for providing too narrow a walkway in the ties-and-socks area.

Tamara had done a good job, Kelly thought, glancing at the ad, then at the displays around her.

"Selected sports jackets, thirty-five to forty percent off," she murmured, then spotted a medium-sized percent-off sign behind a rack of discounted knit shirts. "There they are," she said, then realized that she was speaking out loud to create some noise in the quiet, after-hours store. Occasionally, she could hear voices coming from the direction of the women's department. They would be having a sale tomorrow, also. The sales manager and her assistants must be checking their displays, too, Kelly thought.

She started down the last aisle, looking for and easily finding a table of discounted socks and assorted underwear and a rack of lightweight sweaters from an overseas factory. Not top-grade stuff, but okay for the money, Kelly thought as she examined one of the sweaters. She replaced it on top of one stack, careful not to damage Tamara's painstaking array of colors.

Kelly folded the full-page ad and tucked it inside her sales file, then started for the office.

"Excuse me, but I'm in the market for a new sports jacket," someone said behind her.

Kelly whirled, not recognizing the voice at first, then shaking a chastising finger at Beau Sullivan, who was laughing at her startled reaction. She crossed her arms, hugging the file against her breasts. Just looking at him was all her heart needed to accelerate to double time. Futility engulfed her. How could she keep a sound head on her shoulders when her heart betrayed her at every turn?

"Sorry. I didn't mean to scare a year's growth out of you." He held his arms out from his sides and looked down at his slightly wrinkled white shirt. "I *would* like a new jacket. Care to help me out?"

She glanced around at the dimly lit store. "As you can see, we're closed. Doors open tomorrow morning at ten, and we're having a September Surprises sale. I'm sure you'll find something then."

He came closer, but his attention was on the rack of sports jackets near her. "Right, but couldn't you help me find something now? What difference is a few hours going to make?"

"You could select an item now, but you couldn't pay for it until tomorrow. The registers are closed."

"You could put it back for me, and I'll come around tomorrow and pay for it then." He gave her a disarming smile. "Come on. How about it?"

"I don't wait on customers anymore. I'm the manager."

He propped one hand at his hip and fingered his smooth, clefted chin with the other. "I seem to recall seeing you wait on a gentleman that day we went to lunch."

She had to think a few moments before she remembered. "Oh, him. Well, he's a family friend. I make exceptions in cases like that."

"And like this?" he asked, jabbing his thumb at his chest. "Like this case? What do you say, Kelly? Want to bend a rule or two just for the hell of it?"

Kelly looked away from the devilment in his eyes, but she couldn't shake the temptation he'd planted in her. "Okay," she said with a casual shrug. She went to the rack of jackets, then turned and gave him a swift once-over. "You're a forty-four long, right?"

"R-right!" He swallowed, almost gulped, with surprise. "How'd you guess that so quickly?"

"Practice," she said, flipping through the jackets. "Lots of practice. Do you have a style in mind?"

"How about a double-breasted? I've never had one of those that I can recall."

She looked at him again, measuring his shoulders and waist with her keen eyes. "No, I wouldn't recommend that for you. It wouldn't look bad, but double-breasted blazers are best on shorter men. Besides, that's too many buttons for you to tackle when you're trying to get to your shoulder holster."

"Okay, what *would* you recommend?"

"You like comfort above all else, correct?"

"Right again. You're almost spooky, you know that?"

She laughed, delighted by his offhanded compliments. "Navy blue looks good on you. Try this." She took a jacket off the rack and handed it to him.

He slipped into it and modeled before a three-way mirror. "What do you think?"

Kelly circled him slowly, then stood behind him and studied the fall of the jacket, the fit, the overall appearance. She tugged at the shoulders, then ran her hands down his back, ignoring Beau's suggestive grin. She shook her head and made a flicking motion with her hands.

"No, take it off. It's no good. You need something more..." She didn't finish, but swept another blazer from its hanger. "This. Try this."

"It's the same jacket," he said, handing over the other one, then taking the next offering from her.

"It's not. Close, but not identical."

He shrugged into it and waited for her thorough examination. "Hey, this fits better. Feels better."

"Yes, that's because it's a European cut."

"What's that?"

"It's tapered for the man with wide shoulders and a slim waist." She looked at him again, liking what she saw. "This is a good designer. Notice the full lining, and the filler under the arms. Those are the signs of a well-constructed garment." She stood at his side and raised one of his arms by the wrist. "Brass buttons. That's a good sign, too. Brass or ivory means the manufacturer isn't cutting costs. Take hold of this button." When he did, she said, "See how tightly it's sewn on? You won't lose that button easily."

"You've sold me, Kelly."

She let go of his wrist, blushing when she realized how caught up she'd become in her demonstration. "You don't even know the price."

"Doesn't matter. Like I said, I'm sold." He removed the jacket and handed it over. "I'll come by tomorrow and pick it up."

"I'll put it in my office."

"Fine."

Kelly folded the jacket over her arm and walked to her office, conscious of Beau following her. She would have been a fool not to have caught his other meaning when he said she'd sold him on the blazer. The way he'd said it and the way he'd looked at her when he'd said it made it clear that he also meant he was sold on her. She entered her office and draped the blazer over a hanger. She hooked it on a coat rack behind her desk.

"There," she said, turning to him. He was sitting on the corner of her desk, swinging one long leg at the knee and practicing his lazy smile on her. Her heart fluttered up to the roof of her mouth, and she had to swallow hard to get rid of the sensation. "You'll know where it is, in case I'm not around when you come by tomorrow."

"Yes, about tomorrow..." He smiled broadly, showing even, white teeth. "Tomorrow *night*."

Kelly put the sales folder on her desk, then wondered what to do with her hands, which had suddenly become moist and trembling. "What about it?" she asked, barely able to force anything more than a whisper. What was wrong with her? she wondered as her heart kept up its frantic pace. She ran her hands down the front of her taupe skirt and hoped Beau wouldn't notice how unnerved she was by his smile, his voice, his dangerous appeal. For the first time, she knew the jittery feeling for what it was, pure sexual chemistry. She'd never known it before, but why, oh *why*, did she have to feel it for *this* man?

"Are we still on?"

"On?" She laughed softly, nervously. "Oh, you mean, am I going to answer the door when you ring the bell?"

"Something like that." He crossed his arms, all calm and cool and in control.

"You invited yourself over. That was rude of you." Kelly clasped her hands together tightly in front of her, all quivering and quaking and in a tailspin.

"Rude." He pretended to contemplate the adjective, squinting one eye and gazing reflectively at the ceiling. "Shall I add that to 'arrogant, obnoxious and manipulative'?"

"Yes, please do." She jerked her chin haughtily, realizing she wasn't going to regain her equilibrium, so she might as well make a grand exit. She made it only halfway to the door. Beau stood up, blocking her path. "Move. I'm going home," she ordered.

"What about tomorrow night? Do you like tacos? Tell me what you like."

"I like a man who doesn't play games, doesn't try to unnerve me every chance he gets, and knows when to surrender gracefully."

He caught her by the shoulders, bringing her closer to him. She had to tip her head back to confront the fire in his eyes. "I'm not playing a game, I'm not trying to make you nervous, and there's no such thing as a graceful surrender." He flattened his hands on either side of her head and guided her mouth to his. The contact was hard, quick and as explosive as a bolt of lightning. It cauterized her hurt feelings and started a blaze in her heart. Kelly felt as if smoke must be curling from her lips as Beau lifted his head to stare deeply into her half-closed eyes. She knew he was assessing the aftermath of his kiss, but she didn't care. She felt all aglow.

"Now, quit acting as if you hate me. I don't believe it, and you don't believe it. First you tried to take me lightly, and now you're trying to take me for a fool. How about if you just take me as I am? It might be a nice experience for both of us."

"Oh, Beau," she said, sighing and letting her forehead rest against his chin. "You've worn me down. Okay, okay." She stood straight, shoulders squared, and chin tipped up. "Tacos are fine. I'll expect you at seven." She stepped around him and left the office with what she hoped was a modicum of dignity. She waited until she was outside before she let herself smile.

He was nothing like Ryan, she thought with a delicious thrill of satisfaction. Ryan had never made her toes curl when he'd kissed her.

Six

When Kelly opened the front door at seven o'clock sharp, Beau strode inside, his arms full of grocery bags. He went straight to the kitchen, flinging over his shoulder, "Good evening. You look great. What kind of perfume is that? Smells wonderful. I'll just put this cooler in the refrigerator, okay?"

Kelly laughed at the barrage of comments and questions. "Yes, be my guest."

He put the wine cooler in the refrigerator to chill it, but paused to study the contents before he closed the door. "Is that key lime pie for us? I hope so. It's my favorite."

"Did anyone ever tell you that you're nosy?" Kelly sat on one of the high stools at the counter to watch Beau empty the grocery sacks. Lettuce, tomatoes, two kinds of cheese, hamburger meat, taco shells, tortilla chips, hot sauce, mild cocktail sauce and a six-pack of colas.

"I'm told that all the time," he said. "But it's a compliment to me. After all, I'm a detective, aren't I? I should be nosy."

Kelly propped her chin in her hands, happy to watch him putter around her kitchen. He wore jeans again, but this pair had carnal knowledge of a washing machine. Their pale blue was nearly a perfect match for his short-sleeved knit shirt, which had a wide white stripe running horizontally around him, chest high. His navy-blue tennis shoes squeaked on the tile floor as he darted about the kitchen, opening cabinets and drawers to find a skillet, a bowl, a cheese grater and a knife.

"Do you happen to have an apron I could wear?" he asked. "It's habit. I work better when I don't worry about spills."

"Beside the refrigerator," Kelly said. "There should be two or three hanging there. Take your pick." She resisted the urge to offer her help, although her upbringing called for it. Her mother would faint dead away if she could see Kelly sitting idle while a man prepared dinner all by himself. And he was a guest, at that! Horror of horrors, Kelly thought in the mode of her mother. What's this world coming to when women sit on their fannies while men do the housework?

"What are you thinking about?" Beau asked, noticing her amused expression.

"My mother. She'd pitch a fit if she could see this. Mother doesn't approve of women who let men do *their* work for them. She defines 'women's work' as anything that has to do with the home."

"I never met your parents, did I?"

"I don't think so. They visit once or twice a year. I go to Orlando every couple of months to see them." She traced the swirls in the wood grain countertop with her forefinger. "The only time you might have met them was at my wedding, but you didn't show up for that, did you?"

"No. I was overseas at the time." He opened two cans of cola and handed one to her. "Housework comes naturally to me. My parents, especially my mother, insisted that the girls *and* the boys pitched in and helped. We all did the dishes, laundry, ironing, cooking—you name it."

"Ryan told me," she said, glancing at him before resuming her restless tracing of the wood grain. "But unlike you, he resented it. Before we married, he made it perfectly clear that he wasn't going to do housework or cook. He said he'd had a bellyful of that when he was growing up. Of course, that was okay with me at the time, because my parents raised me to be little Mrs. Suzie Homemaker Extraordinaire. I'd been told that the key to a happy marriage was in being a good housekeeper." She glanced at him again to catch his sad smile.

"If only life were that simple," he said. He heated the skillet, then put in the hamburger to brown. "I never resented housework when I was growing up. Later I was glad to have the experience, since I had to keep my own house, do my own laundry, and so forth."

"Old habits are hard to break. I'm biting my tongue to keep from asking if I can help you do anything."

He laughed, and shook his head. "You can't, so don't ask." He sat at the table to chop up lettuce, grate cheese and slice tomatoes into neat wedges. "I like your house. It feels..." He looked up from his tasks to assess his surroundings. "Solid, permanent. You've got good taste in decor, too. I think a house near the beach should reflect the beach, and this one does. Seashells scattered here and there," he said, noting the touches that hadn't escaped his keen eye. "Open spaces, cool colors, and tropical-style furniture. Very nice. Very Floridian."

THE SECOND MR. SULLIVAN

"Thanks," she said, looking around at her things with a new perspective. "A lot of thought didn't go into this design. It's definitely eclectic. When I moved back here, I moved with only a few items of furniture."

"Weren't you awarded the house and furnishings in the divorce?"

"Yes, but I couldn't keep the house on the money I was making right after the divorce. I had to sell it. As for the furnishings, I sold them, too, to get enough cash together for my move to Miami."

"I guess it was rough at first... being on your own."

"You guess right." She slid off the high stool and sat at the table with him. A tomato wedge tempted, and she plucked it from the cutting board and popped it into her mouth. "I was a babe in the woods. The first few months after the divorce, I swear I was shell-shocked. I don't remember much about that time except for my frequent crying jags and my constant self-pity. I felt guilty, too."

"Guilty over what?"

"Failing in my marriage. I felt as if I'd let my parents down. I took total responsibility for everything. I spent hours and hours going over my married years and trying to figure out what I'd done wrong." She nibbled at a piece of lettuce, remembering the woman she used to be. "But the shock wore off and reality sank in."

"And you pulled yourself up, dusted yourself off and started all over again," Beau said, waving the knife. "Lady, look at you now. You've got a great home, a great job and a great guy like me to cook dinner for you. Life is good, isn't it?" he asked, dipping his head a little to capture her gaze.

Kelly smiled shyly. "Yes, it is," she agreed after a few moments of silent speculation. "Is life good for you, too?"

"Yes, and getting better all the time." He sprang up to stir the seasoned meat, then removed it from the skillet. "Okay, that's done. I'll pop these taco shells and tortilla chips into the microwave and we'll be in business." He went to the cabinets for dinner plates and stemware. He set the table with touching care, although somewhat awkwardly, as if he weren't used to such preparations. He folded the napkins just so and made sure the cutlery and stemware were correctly positioned.

"You're an uncommon man," Kelly said when he'd finished and was rescuing the taco shells and basket of chips from the microwave. He set them on the table along with the other taco ingredients, then took off the apron and put it back on its peg by the refrigerator. "What do you consider to be your specialty dish?" she asked.

"Pancakes."

"Really?"

"I make them as light as crepes."

Kelly constructed a taco while Beau opened and poured the red wine. The tacos were a success, the chips and spicy sauce a perfect accompaniment, and the wine was fruity and refreshing. Kelly served the chilled key lime pie for dessert, and Beau made a fuss over it. He ate two slices and said he might eat a third later. He insisted that Kelly go out and sit on the patio while he loaded the dishwasher. He joined her fifteen minutes later.

"All done. Your kitchen is sparkling clean again," he announced, falling negligently onto the lounger. "Ah, smell that ocean. The breeze feels good tonight. Not too nippy."

Seated in one of the chairs, Kelly propped her bare feet on the railing and laced her hands across her stomach. Her yellow and white seersucker sunsuit left her legs and arms exposed, but she wasn't cold. The wind blowing from the ocean was pleasantly cool. She'd pulled her raven hair into a high ponytail, tied by a yellow satin ribbon. A puff of air fanned her neck.

"If you like my house because it seems solid and permanent, then why don't you buy one like it, instead of living in one on wheels?" she asked after a few minutes of congenial silence.

"I'm thinking along those lines," he admitted. "Before now I was kept on the move because of the jobs I had."

"Why haven't you married?"

"I guess the main reason is that I haven't fallen in love yet." He met her dubious glance with a carefree laugh. "I've been close to it, but not close enough. Besides, I've been traveling so much, and it's hard to develop a serious relationship under those conditions. Most of the women I've known have been intimidated by my independence. I think they felt as if I was the kind of guy who didn't take anyone seriously for any length of time."

"Are you that type of guy?"

"No, I don't think so. Maybe I don't make women feel as if I need them enough. Does that sound cockeyed to you?"

"No." She stood up and stretched. "Let's walk on the beach."

"Okay." He bounded up from the lounger, kicked off his shoes and fell into step with her across the rolling ground, down the gentle slope and finally to the powdery sand. When they'd walked a couple of yards, he casually draped his arm across her shoulders. Kelly made no protest. She'd been expecting it. What she hadn't expected was her own reaction. His hand dangled over her shoulder, and she automatically reached up and laced her fingers through his. He gave a little squeeze, acknowledging the gesture and making Kelly aware of it herself. Funny how natural things seemed with him sometimes, she thought. She couldn't recall being this comfortable with a man since her divorce. Beau's company tonight was easy, friendly, but not platonic. The chemistry was still there, bubbling under the surface.

"I'm surprised that the women you dated were intimidated by your self-sufficiency," she said, circling back to his observation. "That's what I find most attractive about you. You don't need a woman to darn your socks, cook your meals or feed your ego. I find that delightfully refreshing."

"It's a relief to know that you find *something* attractive about me," he said, his voice deepened by amusement.

"Seriously, I envy your independence. I want it so desperately."

"I thought you had it already."

"Not completely," she said. She studied the sand ahead for sharp pieces of shell to avoid stepping on. They had edged closer to the ocean and now were walking along the water line, where the salty ocean rushed onto the gray sand, foamed across their feet, then slipped back into the liquid mass again. "I want to be completely self-reliant. I want to own my home outright so that I'll never have to sell it unless *I* want to."

"No debts, is that it?"

"More than that. You know that I married right out of high school."

"Yes."

"Well, after my divorce, I was woefully unprepared to take care of myself. I thought about moving in with my parents again." She flung back her head, laughing at herself and at Beau's look of horror. "It was a knee-jerk reaction, but I strongly considered it. It took me a year before I realized I was living out of boxes and eating on paper plates because I didn't have anyone to keep house for or cook for, as if *I* didn't count. Isn't that sad? To think so little of yourself?"

"The 'just me' syndrome," he said. He noticed her puzzled glance and explained, "That's when people living alone don't prepare good meals for themselves because 'it's just me.' Or they don't clean their apartments or hang pictures on the walls because 'it's just me living here.' Some people neglect those things out of pure laziness, but when they don't do them because they don't think they deserve the best in life, that's tragic."

"I couldn't agree more. My self-confidence started blooming again when I started doing nice things for myself. I realized that I'd been a good housekeeper and a good helpmate, but I'd been a failure at being my own person. Every once in a while I still feel guilty when I do things for myself, like buying a new outfit just for the heck of it or grilling a sirloin steak just for little ole me."

"Shame on you for feeling guilty."

"You sound like Bette," Kelly said, laughing. "She's been my shining example of independent womanhood since the day we met. I couldn't have selected a better neighbor if I'd tried. The minute I met her, I wanted to be like her. She's the captain of her own life, like you. She has an unusual job, which she takes great pride in, she works around men and is treated as an equal by them, she owns her own home and her own car and her own boat, and she doesn't need anyone in her life. She's happy. Single and satisfied."

"I'm all for being independent, but that doesn't mean you have to exclude everyone from your life."

"I know." Kelly kicked at the sand, tiring of the subject. "Did you always want to be in law enforcement?"

"No, when I was five I wanted to be a cowboy."

"Didn't everyone?"

He chuckled and stopped to roll up the legs of his jeans, then he took her hand in his and continued their stroll. They moved closer to the foaming surf. The water rushed and swirled above their ankles.

"I have two uncles who are cops in Chicago," he said, swinging her hand in his. "I loved hearing their stories about catching the bad guys. By the time I was ready for college, I'd made a nebulous decision to do something in law enforcement. I was a policeman for a short while, but I couldn't stand all the rules, regulations and politics. I earned my master's degree and joined the FBI, but they had just as many rules and regulations—and talk about politics!" He gave a long whistle and shook his head. "The place is rife with it. I joined a bodyguard service and was assigned to a millionaire overseas. That was okay for a while, but I got tired of living abroad. A couple of years ago I worked for an insurance company, and that led to my decision to acquire my detective's license and open my own business."

"How do you like it so far?"

"I have a great boss," he said, grinning broadly. "He's understanding, not demanding, and lets me go home early when I feel like it." He stopped, picked up a flat rock and flung it out into the ocean. "I like it," he said when the rock disappeared under the waves. "I had a good time traveling around and seeing the world, but I'm ready to stay put for a while. I want to belong somewhere. I guess I want a *real* home." He swung his gaze to hers, and a gentle smile nudged the corners of his mouth. "I envy *you* that. I guess you just don't appreciate things until you don't have them."

"I guess so." She was the first to look away, suddenly shy of him. "It's getting colder. Let's start back."

He curved an arm around her shoulders and pulled her against his side on the way back to her house. He had large hands, Kelly noted, glancing sideways at the way his hand completely covered her shoulder and some of her upper arm. Beside him she felt delicate, but not vulnerable.

They were walking into the wind, so they bent their heads and plowed through the air current.

"Where have you been overseas?" she said, speaking over the noisy surf.

"Europe, the Far East, South America, Australia. Lots of places. I took six months off and bummed around."

"Must have been heavenly."

"It was, but I got homesick. There's no better place than this red, white, and blue country."

"Not even France? Italy? Germany?"

He wrinkled his nose playfully. "Nah, they talk funny over there."

She laughed and put her arm around his waist, feeling free to be herself and do what came naturally. Kelly wondered if her misgivings about a personal involvement with Beau had somehow floated away, like shell fragments caught by a wave and taken out to sea.

Back at her house, they put ice cubes in glasses and poured the rest of the wine cooler, which had grown tepid, over them. They sat on the patio, Beau in the lounger and Kelly in the chair. The night closed in around them, sheltering and caressing. The stars and moon provided enough light for them to see each other's expressions, smiles, flashing glances, lingering gazes.

"Do you think you'll ever marry again, Kelly?" Beau asked.

"Possibly, but it will be a different marriage."

"Naturally."

"I mean, I'll approach the next one differently. I won't make the same mistakes."

"No, you'll make different ones."

She started to argue, then realized she couldn't. He was right. Her next marriage wouldn't be perfect either. Just different.

"What do you want out of your next marriage, if there is one?" he asked between sips of the tangy beverage.

"Let me think...." She gazed at the stars and gauzy clouds for a full minute, fashioning her answer before sharing it. "I want equality. I want to feel like a full partner, not just an assistant. And I want a little excitement once in a while!"

"Define 'excitement,'" he requested.

"Oh, nothing big. Surprise parties occasionally. Spur-of-the-moment weekend trips. A rose for no reason. A phone call out of the blue. Things like that."

"There's nothing wrong with those things. They make life interesting." He rolled his head sideways to look at her straight on. "You didn't mention anything about the intimacies. Which is more important to you, quality or quantity?"

"I...I don't know what you mean."

"Well, do you like slow hands or frequent ones, to put it delicately."

"Oh, I see what you're getting at." She looked down into the stemmed glass she held and felt her face glow with embarrassment. "I guess slow ones, if I have to make a choice. Both kinds would be nice." She finished the wine cooler and set the glass beside her chair.

He laughed lustily. "That's the way to think. Why settle when you can have it all?" He finished his drink, too, and put his glass next to hers.

"What things do *you* want out of marriage?" she asked, surprised that she was so avidly curious. Marriage had been a topic she had avoided since her divorce. Opening the subject and discussing it without bitterness or sarcasm were good signs, Kelly thought. It meant that she was truly healing and growing stronger, both emotionally and spiritually. It was a relief to talk about marriage with a sense of hope again, instead of with despair.

"What do I want out of marriage?" he repeated thoughtfully, haltingly. "A kind and loving soul who'll laugh with me, make love with me and make babies with me."

"Children." Kelly smiled, finding his simple, heartwarming request so unlike the Beau she'd heard about years ago.

"You don't approve?"

"I wanted children when I was married, but Ryan said he wasn't ready to father any. In one way, I'm glad we didn't have any, but in another way, I wish we had. Maybe I wouldn't have felt so alone, so abandoned, if I'd had a child from the marriage."

"You would have felt just as abandoned," Beau said. "The only difference would be that you'd feel as if your child was also abandoned."

"Maybe." She shrugged. "It's all hypothetical. Even our hopes for the condition of marriage. Nobody can predict if a marriage will withstand all the trials. There are so many things that can go wrong."

"And so many that can go right," he asserted gently.

"I shouldn't be so negative," she agreed. "Sometimes I get carried away."

"I'll buy a ticket to *that*," he said, sitting up with a burst of enthusiasm that made his green eyes sparkle. "I'd like to see you get carried away."

"Stop it," she said, laughing at his teasing remarks. "I think that wine is going to your head."

"Or you are," he said softly, almost growling.

"Uh-oh," Kelly said, trying to keep things lighthearted. "You've got that crazy look in your eyes."

"Am I making you nervous again? Uncomfortable? I've been walking on eggshells all evening to keep from doing that."

"Have you?" She saw that he was serious. "Well, it worked. I've been as happy as a clam. You've been excellent company."

"That's because I've kept it friendly." He stared moodily across the short, sparse grass to where the ocean roared. He frowned and a crease appeared between his eyes. "I've kept my feelings for you reined in. It hasn't been easy, and it sure as hell hasn't been fun."

"Beau..." She shook her head, unable to think of anything that would help the situation. "If I'd met you when I was in high school—before Ryan—things would be different."

"You mean, if my last name weren't Sullivan, you'd like me a lot better?"

"Not better, but it would be easier. That's for sure."

He dropped to his knees before her and gripped her upper arms. His eyes were dark green, lit by an inner glow. "Then forget my name is Sullivan. Pretend that it's Mud or Charming or whatever you like."

"Beau, get up off your knees," Kelly said, laughing a little but feeling the sexual tug of him. Emotion swamped her as quickly as a flash flood. Had she kept her feelings on a tight rein, too? If she let herself go, would she melt in his arms and beg him to make love to her until dawn? A weakness invaded her, giving her an answer to the questions.

"For just one night, Kelly," he insisted. "For just *this* night, forget that you ever knew me before. Forget I was related to you, in-law or otherwise. Please, Kelly. Just for tonight." He swayed forward, wedging himself between her knees. He looped his arms around her waist and hauled her almost out of the chair and into his lap. He sprinkled tiny kisses from the corner of her eye to the curve of her jaw, then he buried his face against her neck. "Kelly, Kelly," he murmured, rocking his head from side to side. "I want you so. I wish you wanted me only half as much."

She closed her eyes in sweet misery. Oh, what a delightful dilemma, she thought disjointedly, bringing her hands up to discover the sharp outline of his shoulder blades beneath his knit shirt. What's in a name? a voice inside her chided, and she knew the voice came from her heart and not her head. Beau kissed her throat, her chin, her mouth, and his lips were cool and gently persuasive. Kelly tipped her head this way and that, giving him free access. She longed to let her emotions take her on a wild ride with him, but a part of her still held back. A part of her was yet unwilling to accept the consequences tomorrow most surely would bring.

He raised his head long enough to recognize the light of passion in her eyes, then he kissed her again. Differently this time. Not so delicately. This time there was mastery in his kiss. A thrilling kind of assertiveness. He was taking charge. Not taking advantage, just taking the lead she'd given him.

She ran her fingertips along the strong planes of his face, his broad cheekbones, and below them where his skin changed to a sandpapery roughness shadowed by tomorrow's beard. She opened her eyes to slits, watching moonlight move across the russet waves of his hair. She pushed her fingers through his hair, combing it back from his wide forehead, tracing the shape of his ears. He smelled wonderfully clean, with the barest hint of a spicy after-shave wafting from his neck and jawline. Kelly rubbed her cheek against his and whispered his name.

Beau stood up, pulling Kelly with him, then enfolding her in his arms. He pressed warm kisses against her neck, her shoulder. He framed her face in his hands and looked at her as if she were the dearest thing on earth. He groaned, and his mouth captured hers, moist and clinging. Kelly felt the tip of his tongue wet her lips, and then slip inside her warm mouth. The caress was swiftly urgent. Beau began to move, his mouth never leaving hers, and Kelly followed blindly, aware of a twisting, swirling path that moved her inside the house and toward her bedroom. She bumped into something, and Beau murmured a hurried apology, then resumed his long, luscious kiss, which pulled and tugged and propelled her along with him. She sensed that she was inside her bedroom, where it was dark, but not so dark that she couldn't see Beau's face poised just above hers. He smiled, and the dimples in his lean cheeks deepened. His lashes made spiky shadows under his eyes. She felt his hands skim down her sides, then around to cup her hips. The intimacy of his actions bolted through her. Kelly ran her hands up his chest to his shoulders and held on, wondering if she was crazy to let this happen.

"I can see the doubts floating in your eyes," Beau said, holding her more tightly, his fingers kneading her pliant flesh. "For the record, I have no qualms about this, but I am a little nervous."

"You wouldn't be human if you weren't," Kelly said, sliding her hands around to his neck. "I hope I'm doing the right thing."

"Does it feel right?" He kissed her eyelids, then rubbed his nose against hers Eskimo-style.

"Yes," Kelly admitted. "Being with you feels so natural, so *right*."

He closed his eyes slowly, languidly, and began humming ever so softly. To Kelly's delight, he began to dance with her, taking small, slow steps. He pressed close to her, his cheek rubbing against her temple, his hands gliding up to her waist, his lower body undulating ever so suggestively against her. He had a good voice, a clear baritone from what she could surmise from his purring hum. She was so lost in his arms that she gave a little gasp when the backs of her legs made contact with the foot of her bed. Beau bent into her, and she fell backward with a startled laugh. Beau pressed her more deeply into the mattress, although his elbows took most of his upper body weight. He pushed his fingers through her shining hair, found the knotted ribbon and released it. Within moments, her hair was free, curling at her shoulders and around his gentle hands. The simple act sent a spiraling pleasure through Kelly, giving release to her doubts. To hell with tomorrow, she thought, crossing her arms behind his neck and pulling herself up to his sensuous mouth. She loved his mouth and the way his kisses varied from hard and quick to slick and lingering. She slanted her head to the left, then the right, while his tongue mated with hers. Passion flared. Kelly's heart soared, swelled, beat frantically. She felt dizzy, but wonderfully alive and tingling all over. A tightness corkscrewed in the pit of her stomach, and she recognized the sensation. She knew it and was thrilled to have found it again.

"I *do* want you, Beau," she whispered between feverish kisses. "More than you know. More than I can say."

He sprang from the bed to peel his shirt off over his head, then he unfastened his jeans and slid the zipper down while Kelly watched, her eyes huge and luminous in the semidarkness. She rose to her knees in the center of the bed and released the four buttons on the front of her sunsuit. Inching the fabric off her smooth shoulders, she smiled at the ragged way Beau was breathing. His chest rose and fell, and the curling hairs grew damp and darker against his bronze skin. Kelly pulled her arms from the sleeves of the suit and pushed it down to her waist. Then she removed her bra, and that sent Beau back into her arms. She sprawled across the bed with him, rolling and laughing and loving the heat of his skin all over her body.

He kissed her breasts and worked the sunsuit and her panties off her hips and down her legs. She gave a little kick, and she was free of her clothing. Kelly inched her fingers into the waistband of his jeans and moaned impatiently. The time had come, she thought. She wanted to see him, touch him, know him. He sat on the edge of the bed, rising only enough to slide his jeans and underwear off his hips. He flung them aside and turned back around to Kelly. She was given a fleeting glimpse of him, aroused and magnificent, then he fastened his lips around one of her throbbing nipples, and she closed her eyes in sheer ecstasy. He nipped lightly, then suckled until Kelly cried out mindlessly.

He explored her body with lips, teeth and hands. Kelly was shocked at the fire burning within her. She had known arousal. She had known desire. But she had never known this delicious sense of expectation. Beau's mouth, light and cool on her heated skin, made her writhe with impatience. She stroked his sides, muscled and hard, and caressed his buttocks, firm and smooth. He pressed his face into the curve of her neck, and she felt his body tense, then bow as he prepared to complete their union.

"Kelly, Kelly," he said against her skin, moaning in a yearning, heartwrenching way.

Kelly opened up to him, showed him the way and welcomed him with a gasp of sublime pleasure. When he was fully inside her, Kelly's racing pulse exploded. She arched upward, straining for even closer contact. His name burst from her lips as she whipped her head from side to side, caught up in her own avalanche of passion.

Then he began moving, driving, creating a tempo that made her shudder and speak soft, senseless syllables. Her body took on a patina of slick perspiration, matching his, sliding and slipping against him. He was breathless when his final, long stroke surged through Kelly. Her insides liquefied with his deep, quaking release. He said her name with wonder, then settled his lips lightly on hers and smiled. She smiled back, feeling like a purring cat in the lap of satisfaction.

"Once more, with feeling?" he asked, his voice gruffly passionate.

"It'll kill me," she said with an exaggerated groan.

"I doubt that."

She placed lush, juicy kisses on his mouth. "But what a way to go," she said, then laughed huskily.

"Now we know why the French call it 'the little death.'" He slid his lips along the bridge of her nose, then kissed her fervently, his lips sandwiching hers and making them wet. "Do you know what this means to me? Being here with you like this?"

Her throat tightened with emotion she hadn't the courage to express openly. Not yet, anyway. It was too soon, too new. Kelly kissed his chin right on the cleft and slipped her tongue into the place where his razor had left a coarse stubble. "Show me," she said, wrapping her body around his in a lover's embrace. "Show me how much."

Seven

Kelly awoke to the unmistakable aroma of fried sausage... and something else. She sat up in bed, flung her hair out of her eyes with one arm and sniffed again. Syrup. Bubbling, hot maple syrup.

"Pancakes," she said, then swung her legs over the side of the bed with a groan. She cradled her head in her hands for a full minute, getting her bearings, giving her body a chance to awaken, remembering last night. She groaned again and went into the adjoining bathroom for a bracing shower and a few minutes of frantic thinking.

How should she handle this? What should she say to him? What in the world had come over her last night? How could she have succumbed so easily, so blithely?

Before last night, the only man she'd been in bed with was her husband. She didn't know how to think of herself now. Well, she'd had a fling. She'd been a party to a one-night stand. Simple as that. She'd have to learn to live with it. It gave a whole new dimension to the way she perceived herself. She'd had more than one man in her life—in her bed, to be exact. Didn't that make her freer, looser?

Kelly turned off the shower and shook her head furiously, slinging water drops every which way. She rejected the last adjective. She wasn't *looser*. She was just...just...more experienced. That's it! She'd been around a little bit.

But she knew herself well enough to be aware of her own feelings, her own motivations. Undiluted lust hadn't led her into the tryst, nor had sexual liberation had anything to do with it. Kelly Diane Sullivan would never go to bed with a man unless it was to make love with him. Make love. Nothing short of it. She was halfway in love with Beau, or she would never have made it to the bedroom with him.

She groaned again, burying her face in her hands as panic ballooned in her chest. The bare truth did nothing to bolster her courage. She had to face him, but how?

He wasn't the new kid on the block where this sort of activity was concerned. The man had been around the world and back again. He'd seen it all, done it all, had it all. Now she knew why those other women had been intimidated by him. How can one woman compete with so much and so many? she wondered, stepping from the shower and drying herself with a thick towel. One thing was certain: she shouldn't make with the hearts and flowers. He wouldn't like that. She should be cool and collected. It was a morning like any other, except that she happened to have company. No big deal. She was a modern woman and could handle this with aplomb.

Bolstered by her own pep talk, Kelly dressed quickly, half afraid that Beau would barge into the room before she was fully clothed. This sudden modesty was ridiculous, she

THE SECOND MR. SULLIVAN

knew, but she couldn't shake it. Last night he'd seen her all, but she didn't want the same thing to happen in the harsh light of day. She wore white sailcloth shorts and a blue sailor-style shirt. She brushed her hair and splashed on a little perfume. On second thought, she applied a minimum of makeup, telling herself she needed color in her cheeks, or he'd think she was ill. In a way she was, but she didn't want him to know it.

She entered the kitchen and stood unnoticed for a minute. He was busy at the stove, flipping flapjacks, humming happily under his breath, one of her aprons tied around his waist. Her electric coffeepot gurgled. Sausage links sizzled in her skillet. Chilled orange juice sat squarely on the table in her prized crystal pitcher. She'd bought it at a flea market two years ago and had never used it—until now. Beau had taken over her kitchen, her bed, her life!

"Good morning," she said, making him spin around, spatula in hand.

"Good morning, morning glory!" He was happy as a lark. Cheerful, chipper, contagious. "You're beautiful, but are you hungry?"

She nodded and slid into one of the chairs at the table. "This pitcher happens to be an antique." She poured herself some orange juice—carefully. "I never use it."

"Why have it, then?"

"To look at. Appreciate."

He shrugged. "I'll hand-wash and dry it. I'll treat it like a new baby." He turned back to the stove. "Happy now?"

"Yes," she said, mollified, but feeling a trifle petty. "You're making your famous pancakes, I take it."

"That's right. Just for you." He placed a platter of sausage links on the table. "I hope you don't mind that I've made myself at home. I was going to wake you, but you looked so sweet that I didn't have the heart. I tiptoed out of the room and got busy in here. There's nothing like a good breakfast after a night in heaven, don't you think?"

"I ... I ..." She shrugged, not knowing *what* to think. "Are you always this industrious in the morning?"

"Not always." He glanced at her. She was drinking the juice as if each tiny sip were an effort. "Are you feeling okay? You look a little peaked."

"How wishy-washy of you. A minute ago I was beautiful!" She waved a hand, dismissing the question. "I'm fine." She got up and went to the cupboard for her favorite mug and filled it with the freshly perked coffee. She added milk, then took the mug back to the table with her. The coffee revived her, burning away the haze in her brain.

He set a plate of pancakes in front of her, and she gulped. Her eyes grew wide to take in the mountain of thin cakes.

"I can't eat all these," she protested, setting the coffee mug down with a thump. "Haven't you ever heard of a *short* stack? Take some of them for yourself."

"Don't be so hasty. Once you taste them, you'll consume them." He sat behind a pancake hill of his own. "Here's the butter," he said, scooting the plastic tub across the table toward her. "Smear on plenty of that, then pour on the hot syrup."

"Beau, I know how to prepare my own pancakes," she said, sweetly sardonic. "My mother taught me a long, long time ago."

"Are you always in a foul mood in the morning?"

"Only when I'm treated like a five-year-old."

"Sorry!" He held up his hands in a surrender, then began doctoring his own stack. "Good loving has a strange effect on you."

"Can we shelve that topic until after I've eaten?"

"Certainly," he said sharply, succinctly. "No problem." He grabbed up the morning paper, unfolded it and hid behind it.

Kelly cut through the stack of pancakes and tasted the rich concoction. She lifted her brows as a wave of culinary pleasure washed over her taste buds.

"Ummm, these *are* wonderful," she said, talking around the light, buttery creation. "So light. You're right. They're more like crepes." She smiled when he lowered the newspaper to reveal his gloating grin. "You're a great cook, Beau, and I'm sorry for being such a grouch this morning. I—well, I thought you'd be long gone by the time I woke up. I never dreamed you'd still be here—and cooking my breakfast, at that!"

"Long gone?" He laid the newspaper aside to give her his full attention. "Why would I leave without letting you know?"

She shrugged, feeling cornered by his gentle probing. When he was this serious, this concerned, this prying, it made her feel all twitchy, as if she were a tiny specimen under a huge microscope.

"I enjoyed last night. Didn't you?" he asked, looking closely for every nuance.

"Of course, but that was last night. I'm back to the old me this morning."

"Who was in bed with me last night?" He kept eating, but she wasn't sure he was tasting anything.

She continued eating for a few minutes, biding her time while she formulated an acceptable answer. "Last night I did something I've never done before." At his dubious glare, she laughed. "Not *that*," she said, reading his mind and knowing that his thoughts were focused on the physical, while hers were on the emotional. "I acted purely on my feelings. I'm not a spontaneous person by nature."

"And?" he goaded when she lapsed into an uneasy silence.

"And it wouldn't be a good idea to continue in that vein."

"Life isn't all or nothing, Kelly." He mopped up the last drops of syrup in his plate with a forkful of pancakes. "Sometimes you go with your feelings; sometimes you don't."

"That's true, but I need to concentrate on my work. I want to stand on my own two feet and not depend on anyone. You understand. You're an independent operator, so I'm not telling you anything new."

He threw down his napkin, stood up and started stacking the dishes. "I told you last night that independence has nothing to do with shoving everybody out of your life. That's selfishness—foolishness—but it's got nothing to do with self-reliance." He took the dishes to the counter, stacking them there, then loaded them one by one into the dishwasher.

Kelly took the last sausage from the platter, ate it, then gathered the rest of the dishes and took them to him. "You've kept people at arm's length all your life. You hardly ever saw your family while I was in it."

"What do you know about how I've lived?" he demanded, almost growling with irritation. He didn't look at her but remained bent over as he loaded the dishwasher.

"You drifted in during holidays, made your obligatory visit, which never lasted more than a couple of hours, and then you vanished. You've always been aloof and untouchable."

"Was I aloof and untouchable last night?"

"No, but we're talking about life, not just one night. You're here one day and gone the next, never staying around long enough to be tied to a place or a person. That's you, Beau. Why deny it?"

"That's *your* version of me," he said, slamming shut the dishwasher and punching a button to send the machine into a wash cycle. He grabbed up the pitcher and took it to the sink to wash and dry it as promised.

"Okay, what's *your* version?" she taunted, leaning against the counter and crossing her arms in a condescending fashion.

"I didn't hang around during holidays for the same reason a bachelor doesn't go to a baby shower."

"I don't get it," Kelly said.

He came to her, thrusting his face close to hers and speaking through clenched teeth. "I didn't fit in."

She inched back her head. "Didn't fit into your own family? That's ridiculous."

"I was—still am—a lone wolf among a clan of couples," he said, teeth still grinding together. "I was envious. I felt estranged. Holidays were the pits for me, especially when husbands received gifts from wives while I accepted presents from my mom and dad like some over-the-hill adolescent." He removed the apron from around his middle and flung it aside. "I'm going to take a run on the beach. Want to join me?"

"No, I don't usually..." She shrugged. "Exercise isn't my thing."

"Suit yourself." He took his shirt off and went out to the patio. He dropped his shirt onto the lounger, then bounded down the steps and jogged to the beach.

Kelly went outside, watching him until he disappeared from view. She was dumbfounded by his heartfelt admission. She'd never once put herself in his shoes, but now that she wore the same style, she knew what he was talking about and how he must have felt around his family.

The Christmases since her divorce had been days for her to get through, not to celebrate. The other day she'd found herself dreading Thanksgiving. Would she stay home or visit her parents? Both prospects depressed her.

She shouldn't have assumed that Beau's discomfort would be any less than hers, she thought. He was privy to the same emotions as she, the same dreams, ambitions, failures. Because Ryan had bounced back so quickly, so cheerfully, after their divorce, Kelly had altered her opinion of men. She'd decided that they were made differently not only outside but inside as well. They didn't form fierce attachments. They didn't feel pain. When you cut them they didn't bleed.

Now she realized that those sweeping generalizations were not only unkind but unfair. She kicked off her shoes and ran to the beach. Beau was circling back to the house, his bare feet sinking into the wet sand, then pulling up clumps of it as he sprinted in her direction. He looked like a coppery-skinned, divinely muscled Adonis. The kind of man that dreams were made of, Kelly thought with a little sigh. Heaven only knew that she'd had her share of dreams about him lately. She didn't regret her night of lovemaking with him, but she was wary of any further attachments. She didn't know how close Beau was to Ryan, and she didn't want to stand between two brothers. Beau had already admitted that he'd spoken to Ryan about her and that Ryan had given her his stamp of approval—that *still* irritated her to no end. Being discussed by them, being a woman they had in common, just couldn't work! Why didn't Beau admit that? Why couldn't he leave well enough alone? They'd shared a beautiful night of lovemaking, and Kelly didn't want to spoil it by continuing a relationship that was doomed. No matter what Beau said, he was still a Sullivan. Last night she'd pretended it wasn't so, but she couldn't keep pretending that there were no clouds on their horizon.

He came huffing and puffing to her. He stopped, propped his hands against his knees and leaned over until he caught his breath.

"Feel better?" she asked.

"Not really." He lifted his arms above his head and stretched, then nodded in the direction of her house. "I'll get my things and get out of your way."

"You're not in my way," Kelly said, walking beside him. "Quit pouting."

"I'm not pouting," he said angrily. "I'm just trying to figure you out."

She curled her fingers in the crook of his arm. He tensed and shook off her hand. "Beau! Why are you being like this? Look, I understand what you were talking about before. Holidays have become a drag for me, too."

"That's *not* what I was talking about before," he said, then trotted up the stairs and inside the house.

Kelly followed him, frowning at his biting tone. He pulled on his shirt, then wet a cloth and began wiping off the table and counter.

"You don't have to do that," Kelly said.

"I want to. I'm a clean freak, especially when I'm upset." He sprinkled scrubbing powder in the sink and set to work on the stains there.

"I'm sorry for upsetting you," Kelly said. "But I wish you'd try to see my viewpoint. Just because I indulged in a delicious whim last night doesn't mean I should make a habit of it."

He'd rinsed out the sink and was drying his hands when he turned to face her. Fury darkened his eyes and pulled at the corners of his mouth. He threw aside the towel in a savage motion.

"Thanks for putting me in my place, Kelly," he said, his voice low and vibrating with anger. "It's nice to know that I'm nothing but a diversion, an experiment, a *whim*."

"Beau, that's not what I meant."

"Well, that's what you said!" He slipped on his watch, then looked around in a quick search. "I'm out of here."

"Beau, don't leave like this," Kelly pleaded, grabbing his arm when he started past her. "Please, Beau. I didn't mean to hurt your feelings."

"So you admit that I have feelings?" He smiled, but it was more like a grimace. "Gee, thanks." He fixed his gaze where her hand rested on his arm. She removed it. "See you around, honey." He feigned concern when she stiffened at his offhanded endearment. "What's wrong? I'm only living up to your image of me. The callous playboy who loves 'em and leaves 'em." He gave a wicked, lecherous wink. "You were great, baby. Maybe I'll call you again sometime."

"Get out!" Kelly ordered.

"With pleasure!" he yelled back at her.

But when he drove away, Kelly went to the door and fought back her tears. She deserved that uncharacteristic behavior, she told herself. She'd sold him short. She'd cheapened what they'd shared by calling her part in it a whim.

She'd been so caught up in her own motivations and reactions that she'd forgotten about his. The wandering playboy couldn't be dismissed so lightly, she thought. He was complex and intense and deserving of her respect. She promised herself that she'd treat him with more kindness.

That won't be hard to do, she thought, closing the front door and dropping in the nearest available chair. Especially since she was falling in love with him.

THE SECOND MR. SULLIVAN

Kelly sighed heavily and closed her eyes. Yes, she was perilously close to adoring him, doting on him, loving him heart and soul. And she couldn't let that happen! Could she?

The activity outside her office brought Kelly's head up from the price lists spread out around her. She could see Tamara, who was speaking to someone obscured from Kelly's view by a shirt form.

"Kelly's busy right now. Can I help you?" Tamara asked, her voice floating through the open office door.

"She'll see me," a man said, and his voice galvanized Kelly.

Kelly stood up, her breath caught in her throat, her hands clenching and unclenching at her sides. "Ryan," she said as her ex-husband entered the office with Tamara right behind him. "What are you doing here?"

He sent a supercilious glare to Tamara, a gesture that Kelly thought of as vintage Ryan. He was astute at making others feel inferior or out of line. Tamara, resplendent in her fifties outfit of poodle skirt, white shirt with Peter Pan collar, bobby socks and saddle oxfords, glared back at him with solid self-assurance.

"I'm sorry, Kelly. Mr. Sullivan wouldn't wait until I could announce his request to see you," Tamara said coldly, leaving no doubt that she was in the right and Ryan was a rude boor.

"Thank you, Tamara. I'll handle this." Kelly waited for her assistant to leave the office before she looked at Ryan again. Kelly noted that he was back to fighting weight. No more spare tire. "Okay, Ryan, what's the meaning of this?"

"Of what?" he tossed back at her. "I simply dropped by for a brief visit. Why is everyone here making a federal case out of it?"

"Probably because you barged in here as if you had a right—which you don't." She motioned to the chair in front of her desk. "Have a seat. I can give you a few minutes."

He gave her a puzzled look, then sat down. Kelly bit her lower lip to keep from grinning. She knew by the confusion he'd showed that Ryan had noticed a difference in her. In the old days she would have been apologetic and demurring. Never so bold and brassy. Well, he was in for further shocks, Kelly thought with a twinge of malice. She was no longer a simpering shadow. She was her own woman, and she didn't need Ryan Sullivan to tell her how to live her life, who to like, what to wear, what to say or how to feel. Not anymore!

"So you manage this department," he said, unbuttoning his jacket and draping his lean body in the office chair. His strawberry-blond hair was shorter than it had been three years ago but still full and lustrous. He was lightly tanned and liberally freckled.

"Yes, I'm sales manager," Kelly said, wondering what he was doing here. "Did you have something to say to me?" she asked, feeling in her heart that his visit had something to do with Beau. "If so, say it. I've got a lot of work to do."

He laughed, but it was forced and vengeful. "Well, time hasn't improved your personality. I'm amazed that you've moved up in this company by being so rude and abrupt with people."

"You're not 'people,'" Kelly said, laughing lightly at him. "You're my ex-husband. I'm sure you're amazed that

THE SECOND MR. SULLIVAN

I've been given a position of authority, since you always treated me like a dimwit."

"I did not!" he said, raising his voice.

"Whatever," Kelly said, waving off his indignation. "Just tell me what you want."

"I don't want anything, and I resent your implication that I'm out to get something from you. I simply stopped by to see how you're doing. I was...concerned."

"Ryan, it's been almost three years and I haven't seen or heard a peep from you. Why now?"

"Why not?" He shrugged broadly.

"Very well." Kelly shuffled papers, tired of his game. "I'm fine. You can go now."

"Kelly," he said, leaning out of his chair to lay his hand on her arm. "Let's bury the hatchet."

"I already have," she said, completely honest. "Haven't you?"

"Yes, but I sense hostility."

"No, Ryan. What you sense is impatience. I'm busy. I didn't get this far in the company by entertaining guests during working hours."

He sat back and studied her carefully. "You've changed," he surmised. "I guess that's all right."

Kelly laughed, throwing back her head as she was seized with mirth. Ryan didn't join in. He sat and watched her, brooding and looking a little miffed at being laughed at by his ex-wife. Kelly sought a more sober countenance.

"Sorry, Ryan. That struck me as funny."

"So I noticed." His voice was clipped. He looked out the glass walls at the department. "Seeing anyone?"

Kelly was suddenly as sober as a judge. "You mean Beau?"

He swung his gaze back to her. "Yes. So, you're still seeing him?"

"What's it to you?" she shot back, not pleased with his interference. It was what she had dreaded the most. Ryan Sullivan was sticking his nose in her business again, and that was the main reason why loving his brother was out of the question for her. "Let me answer that," she said before he could respond. "It's none of your business who I see or what I do when I'm with them. You got that, Ryan?"

"Loud and clear, and I agree completely." He fixed an earnest expression on his face. "Really, Kelly. I think it's great that you're getting your life back together."

"I've got it back together," she corrected. "I'm happier than I've ever been in my life."

"That's great!" He bounded up from the chair, his body tense with sincerity. "I'm all for it."

"All for what?" Kelly asked, rising slowly like a plume of smoke.

"Did you know that I'm being transferred?"

"I...what?" She shook her head, trying to follow his conversation. "No. Why should I know about something like that?"

"Oh, right. Well, I've accepted a manager's position at the home office in Seattle."

"Seattle?" Kelly repeated, thinking that Seattle was her second choice, right after the moon. "Good. Congratulations." She held out her hand, smiling politely when Ryan hesitated before he shook it. "When will you be moving?"

"In the next couple of weeks."

"Well, good luck." She came around the desk, making no pretense of showing him to the door. "Thanks for stopping by and telling me."

"Kelly, wait." He lifted his elbow from her guiding hand. "There's one other thing." He gathered a deep breath and smiled. "I want you to know that you and Beau have my blessing."

"Your blessing?" Kelly stepped away from Ryan, afraid that being close to him was too much of a temptation. She'd like nothing better than to slap his face. "Ryan, I didn't ask for, nor do I need, your blessing. If I want to continue to see your brother, I'll do it, whether you like it or not!" She was shaking with anger, incensed by his unmitigated gall.

"There's no call for you to be so hateful! I'm being nice. I was trying to make you feel better."

"Don't try so hard. Just stay out of my life!"

Kelly and Ryan saw Beau at the same time. He was standing just outside the office, watching their display of hot emotions with a cool smile. They both froze and stared, white-faced and shaking, at him. Beau looked from one to the other, then stepped gingerly into the office as if he were afraid of land mines.

"I thought I recognized your voices as they carried across the entire department store," Beau said, draping one arm around his brother's shoulders. "Mom called me this morning and said that you were moving to Seattle. That promotion came through, huh? Well, great! Let me buy you a drink. There's a nice pub a block from here." Beau glanced at Kelly, and an understanding smile touched his mouth, then was gone. The silent communication told her that he was saving her from any further confrontation. "I'd ask you along, Kelly, but I know you're busy."

"Yes, I am." She went back to her desk and sat down. "You two go on and have a good time."

"You heard her, Ryan," Beau said, turning Ryan around and marching him out of her office. "Maybe you'll be so busy with your new job that you won't have time to meddle in other people's lives, little brother."

"I resent that!" Ryan blustered, but Beau just laughed and caught him in a playful headlock. Ryan wiggled out of the wrestling hold, then laughed under his breath and went along peacefully.

Kelly sat back, blowing up at her bangs, lifting them briefly from her forehead. She tossed aside the pen she'd been holding and held her head instead. Ooh, those Sullivan men! Were they her curse or her ultimate challenge?

Eight

Curiosity killed the cat, but that didn't stop Kelly from driving by Beau's place on her way home from work. She'd expected him to drop by later that afternoon and discuss his visit with Ryan, but there had been no sign of him. Kelly tried to put it out of her mind, but she kept wondering about what Beau might have discussed with Ryan and vice versa. Then she started worrying that Beau might be avoiding her because of something Ryan had said or implied. Her imagination running amok, she parked in front of Beau's motor home and got out of her car. He was washing the outside of his home, and he paused briefly to acknowledge her presence.

Foot Long barked, then shook herself all over. She'd been shampooed recently, and she was still damp. Kelly recalled Beau's comment that he cleaned things when he was upset. She watched him take a wet mop and wipe furiously at the film of dirt on the outside of the motor home. She ducked her head to hide her smile.

"What brings you here?" he asked, glancing at her as he dunked the rag mop into the tub of sudsy water, then wrung it out with his hands.

"I'm just being neighborly," she said, bending over to pet Foot Long.

"Right," he said, making it two syllables, spanning an octave. His glance was pure skepticism.

"So you're still upset with me," she said, tapping the toe of her shoe against the mop bucket and landing her own low blow.

He stopped mopping to deliver a thunderous glare. "I'm not cleaning because I'm upset with you. I think better when I'm busy."

"Right," she said, imitating his earlier delivery. "What are you thinking about?"

"Business."

"Mall business?"

"Yes."

She sighed, having been briefed on the latest developments by Joe Cauley before she'd left the mall. "I heard about it. Mr. Cauley said that three other mall employees have been hit by the credit-card culprit."

"And the heat is on," he said, pausing to wipe perspiration from his brow with the back of his hand. "The mall 'shirts' are leaning on me. They want results—quick."

"What are 'mall shirts'?" she asked.

"Cop talk. 'Shirts' are the guys giving the orders. 'Suits' are the elected officials or chief executive officers."

"What are you?"

"Me? I'm just a 'regular.' Nothing fancy. Just another working stiff."

"The guy who gets things done?" Kelly asked, smiling at him.

"That's right." He smiled back. "And that's why I'm thinking hard today. I've got to break this case before it breaks me."

"Any bright ideas?"

"Maybe." He stood back to admire the shine he'd put on his motor home. "How would you like to see my office?"

"I'd love it." She sent him a questioning look, then laughed. "Does this mean we're friends again?"

"Let's go into town and take it from there." He looked down at his damp clothes. "I'll just take a few minutes to shower and change."

"Go ahead. I'll stay out here with Foot Long."

Beau was in and out of the motor home within twenty minutes, looking wonderfully virile, rugged and devil-may-care as a breeze ruffled his hair and made his shirt billow out, then hug his wide chest.

"Shall we take my car?" he asked, patting his back pocket to make sure he'd remembered his wallet and keys.

"Okay," she said, already moving toward it.

He locked Foot Long inside the motor home, then settled into the driver's seat and secured his safety belt. "I guess you're wondering about what happened after I left your office today."

"Thanks for coming by when you did. Your timing was perfect."

"Do you and Ryan always go at each other like that?"

"Believe it or not, Ryan and I rarely raised our voices to each other during our marriage."

"So why was today different?" he asked, rolling down the window to let in a cool breeze.

"The day wasn't different. *I'm* different."

They entered St. Augustine and Beau drove to the heart of town.

"By different, do you mean you're more vocal than you used to be?" Beau asked.

"I'm more vocal, more opinionated, more self-confident, more *everything*."

He parked the car in front of an office building and turned sideways to look at her, then at the structure behind her.

"This is it?"

"This is it," he confirmed, unfolding his tall frame from the car. "Good location, isn't it?"

"Couldn't be better," she agreed as he came around the front of the car. She linked her arm in his. Once again she was struck by the confidence she felt with him. Normally she wouldn't take a man's arm until it was offered, but with Beau she followed her instincts.

He led her upstairs to his office, then stood back so that she could get the full effect of seeing his name emblazoned upon the door. Kelly gave him his due, widening her eyes and releasing a gasp of pleasure.

"My, my! Aren't we important!" she teased, making him grin from ear to ear as he unlocked the door, pushed it wide open and extended an arm inside.

Kelly went into the small office and glanced around, noting the neat desk with its silver appointments, oak file cabinets and framed documents on one wall.

"It's small and kind of impersonal, but then again it's small and kind of impersonal," he joked, tossing his keys onto the desk and leaning against the edge of it.

"It's larger than my office, so don't complain." She made a slow journey around the room, then sat in one of the chairs in front of his desk. "What you really need is a hat rack for your homburg."

"I don't have a homburg."

"Every detective worth his salt should have one," she said. "Don't you watch the late movie?"

"Then I should have a trench coat to go with it."

"Absolutely!" She imagined him in such an outfit and smiled. "You'd be nothing short of dashing in that get-up."

"And a teensy bit conspicuous," he added, lifting one brow in a gentle rebuff. "Private detectives are supposed to melt into the woodwork, not stand out like a cherry on a cream pie."

Her instincts were at work again, and Kelly obeyed them by rising from the chair and taking the two steps that brought her right in front of him.

"Then you're in trouble," she said, hearing the husky tone of her voice and wondering what it was about Beau Sullivan that made her blood simmer. "Because I can't imagine you ever melting into the woodwork." She laid her hands on his shirtfront, and his hands came up automatically to cover them.

He tipped his head to one side and his lips slanted across hers. He brought her hands around his waist and then placed his upon her hips to guide the lower part of her body between his legs. His lips trailed fire down the side of her neck, then he bit lightly at her shoulder. Kelly laughed and leaned back to look into his sparkling eyes.

"What else did Ryan say?"

He frowned and kissed her again. "How dare you bring up his name when I'm doing my best to seduce you."

"You don't have to try very hard," she said. "For some reason, I'm about as solid as Jell-O around you."

"I love to hear that," he admitted, then glanced up as he shifted his thoughts from her to her earlier question. "What did Ryan say... Oh, right. He said you'd changed.

He said you seemed defensive, almost as if you were spoiling for a fight."

"Maybe I was...." She thought for a few moments as she unconsciously ran her hands up and down Beau's back. "No, I wasn't looking for a fight," she said decisively. "I tried with all my might to be courteous, but Ryan surprised me. I never expected to see him there."

"He wanted to tell you himself that he's leaving Florida." Beau left her arms to cross the office and stand by the window. He opened the miniblinds and stared out. "He says that he wishes you all the best, and I believe him." Beau turned sideways and his eyes held a wicked gleam. "The best, of course, is me."

Kelly smiled but decided not to comment on his deduction. "I hope Ryan will be happy in Seattle."

"He'll be fine."

"So will I." She shrugged. "I'm glad he's leaving."

"I know." Beau grinned crookedly. "Ryan didn't think you'd be brokenhearted about it."

"Didn't you feel weird talking about me with him?"

"No."

"He's my ex-husband! I would think you'd be very uncomfortable."

"That's because you act as if you and I are blood related, when our past connection is, at best, negligible."

"Negli—" She bit off the rest of the word and placed a hand to her forehead in confusion. "I don't believe that you're as nonchalant about this as you're pretending to be. Any *normal* human being would have felt peculiar in the situation."

"Did you just call me abnormal?"

"No." She sighed. "I didn't mean to, anyway."

"Look, I didn't talk about you that much when I was with Ryan." He came to her and took her hands in his.

THE SECOND MR. SULLIVAN

"Ryan talked. I listened. He wanted to be sure that I understood why he'd dropped by to see you. Ryan wants you to be happy, Kelly. I think he feels guilty, and it will ease his conscience if you take up with a nice guy. Like me." He grinned and squeezed her hands, making her blush. "I have a feeling that what really rankles you is that Ryan knows a little bit about what's going on in your life."

"That's right." She averted her gaze, unable to look him in the eyes when she admitted he was on the right track. "When I was married, Ryan ran my life. I don't want him involved in my world anymore. There's no place for him in it."

"What do you mean, he ran your life?"

"It's not right for me to talk about your brother," she argued, then jumped slightly when he let go of one of her hands to bring her face around to his. She sighed expansively as he pressed full kisses from the corner of her eye to the corner of her mouth. "Beau, please... I can't think when... oh, Beau. This is so complicated."

"No, it isn't." He looked deeply into her eyes, seeking the truth and her trust. "Talk to me. I want to understand."

"Talking about him isn't easy. I've made it a practice to keep my past private." She stepped into his arms, pressed her cheek against his chest and closed her eyes. She felt safe, secure, and her resistance dissolved. "I tried to be perfect for Ryan, but I never was," she confided as Beau's arms tightened around her and his lips moved against her hair. "That's what I like about you. You don't try to change me all the time. Ryan was so critical. He had an uncanny ability to make me feel unworthy, inferior. He criticized my hair, my clothes, my political views, my opinions of films and books. Everything!"

"I know how bossy Ryan can be. He tried to boss me, but I usually cut him down to size. After all, he's my little brother. I couldn't let him get the best of me."

"I was easy to manipulate," Kelly said, wincing at the memories.

"I can't imagine you letting anyone bulldoze you."

"That was then. This is now." She felt stronger, so she stepped out of his arms and went to stand by the window. "Like I said before, I'm different. Back then, I was putty in his hands. I'd been brought up to think that was the way a marriage worked. The husband made the decisions. The wife went along."

"That's the dark ages, honey."

She looked over her shoulder at his tender smile, and her heart filled with love for him. "I know," she admitted, looking forward again as he came up behind her and slipped his arms around her waist.

"It's strange that he married a career woman the second time around," Beau said, pulling Kelly back against him.

"Not really. He grew tired of what he'd created. A woman who didn't need him to think for her was exciting to him. It's a natural reaction, when you think about it. I was perfectly happy with the way things were. I cooked, cleaned, ran errands and socialized when it helped Ryan's career. But I was living a child's existence. I put myself in an adult's hands and let him conduct the business of life for me. I felt fortunate to have a husband like Ryan, and I pitied those poor women who had to work outside the home. I blamed the growing number of divorces on two-career marriages, so you can imagine my shock when my perfect setup crumbled."

"When did you realize your marriage was in trouble?"

She took a deep breath as the past crowded in around her. "Ryan started talking about this other woman. A woman he met through his work. I should have known that he was attracted to her, but I didn't suspect anything. But then Ryan became even more critical of me. I couldn't do anything to please him. I was frantic."

"Easy, easy." He rubbed the side of his face against hers. "Was this other woman named Ashley?"

"No, she came later—after the divorce." She felt his surprise and smiled. "The woman's name isn't important. Of course, I have no respect for women who have affairs with married men, but obviously Ryan's commitment to me had weakened, or another woman couldn't have broken it. The irony is that I was trying so hard to be what Ryan wanted, and the other woman was my exact opposite. Like Ashley, she was involved in her career and had an independent spirit."

"Now that's what you've become."

She shook her head, and leaned back against him. He felt wonderful. Solid, long, lean. Her blood began to simmer again, and she closed her eyes to focus her thoughts away from the physical.

"That's what I always should have been," she said. "Being responsible for yourself, accepting and knowing your own strengths and weaknesses, not relying on anyone else to make you happy—these are characteristics of adulthood. I wasn't a wife; I was Ryan's little girl."

"I think you're being too hard on yourself."

"Maybe, but I've had to get tough. When the marriage collapsed, I found myself in a world I knew nothing about. I had no training, no earthly idea of how to handle my own finances and no inkling of how to apply for work. I was my own worst enemy, because I didn't think I was qualified for anything. I went to job interviews knowing I wouldn't get the job. I had no confidence in myself."

"That's hard for me to imagine," he admitted. "You're such a go-getter now."

"Actually, my divorce was good for me. The adjustment was hell, but the payoff was worth it." She tipped her head back against his shoulder. "You're the easiest man to be around," she said, sighing with relief. She felt as if she'd lifted a hundred-pound weight off her chest. "I've made it a practice never to discuss my divorce with other men, but here I am telling you the whole, sordid story."

"I asked."

"Yes, but so have others."

"Have there been many others?"

She crossed her arms against his at her waist. "What a leading question!" She made him wait a few more seconds before she answered. "I've dated frequently, but not seriously."

"Do you have something against serious relationships?"

"No." She was suddenly defensive. "Why do you ask?"

"Because you seem to give just so much of yourself, then you pull away. Do you always do that, or just with me?"

She wrenched from his arms, giving herself room to face him. "You're imagining things."

"I wonder." He fingered his chin and squinted his eyes. "You know what you just did? You pulled away when I probed too close."

"No, I—" She cut off the denial, realizing that he was right. Kelly laughed softly at herself. Did a person ever fully know oneself? she wondered. Or did one evolve constantly, making it impossible to know every corner, every nuance of one's own personality? "I guess you're right," she admitted. "I did pull away. Once burned, twice shy, or so the saying goes." She turned aside swiftly when he started toward her. "Yes, I like this office," she said, trying to ward him off with a change of subject. "You need a secretary to make it complete. Some blond gum-chewer with a high voice and a beauty mark."

He went past her and sat on the couch. It sagged in the middle, so he sat on one end of it.

"No, I'd rather have a dark-haired beauty with a great smile. Ms. Sullivan, come here and take a letter." He pointed at his lap. "Please?"

She recognized the challenge. It was clear in his voice and his eyes. He was asking her to quit pulling away, to open up to him completely. For a few moments, she was immobilized by the restraints she'd attached to herself after her divorce, but then she broke free of them. She sat in Beau's lap, looped her arms around his neck and wiggled to a more comfortable position. He grimaced playfully, gritted his teeth and sucked in his breath.

"Do that again and I won't be responsible for my actions, Ms. Sullivan."

"I'm sorry for being so guarded," she said, resting her forehead against his. "Old habits are hard to break."

"I forgive you." His lips reached out for hers, touched, then drew back. "So, do you really like my office?"

"Yes, but why do you have a couch in here?"

"For moments just like this," he said, sliding her back off his lap and onto the cushions. "I've dreamed of getting you in here and on this couch."

"You didn't," she said, laughing.

"I did!" He helped her recline full-length on the couch, then he stretched out on top of her. "Now, Ms. Sullivan, please pay careful attention to my dictation, because I might ask you to repeat it."

"Yes, sir." She tipped back her head as he bent toward her. His mouth slipped down to the base of her throat. She kicked off her dress sandals and pulled his shirt free of his waistband.

Beau straightened to one knee and unbuttoned his shirt so that she could touch him. She curled up, placed a hand at the back of his neck and brought his mouth to hers in a kiss that left no doubt of her feelings for him. She wet his lips with her tongue. He pressed her down again onto the slip-covered couch. It creaked but then made no further complaint.

Kelly caressed his ribs, the soft covering of hair on his chest, the smoothness of his back. She stroked him, urging him on while her mouth grew hot upon his. His tongue swept inside, sliding back and forth. The message was clear. He wanted her, and she wanted him. Here. Now.

He wedged his thigh between her legs and began unbuttoning her blouse. His mouth was slick upon her shoulder and on the tops of her breasts. She grasped his belt, unbuckled it and her fingers closed on the zipper pull tab.

Someone knocked on the office door, and they both froze and stared at each other in a few moments of sheer panic.

"Beau? Beau, are you in there?"

"My parents!" he mouthed, then bounded to his feet. He buttoned his shirt, stuffed it into his waistband, buckled his belt, handed Kelly her sandals. His movements were too swift to follow. "What in hell are they doing here?" he whispered, staring at the bobbing shadows on the other side of the frosted glass door panel.

"Beau? It's Mom and Dad."

"Right," he called, making a gesture to hurry Kelly as she adjusted her clothing. "Wait a sec. I'm on the phone." He ran his hands through his hair, waited for Kelly's jerky nod, then unlocked the door and opened it. "Hi! What are you two doing here?"

Kelly sat stiffly on the couch, her hands clutched in her lap, a wooden smile on her lips. She wondered if she looked as guilty as she felt. Guilty for what? a reasoning voice asked in her mind. Of loving their son? What's so terrible about that? You didn't feel guilty when you loved Ryan. She raised her gaze to Mrs. Sullivan's sweet smile.

"Hello, Kelly. It's so good to see you again."

"It's good to see you, too," Kelly said truthfully. "Hello, Mr. Sullivan."

Beau's father patted Kelly's shoulder. "Good to see you, dear. How have you been?"

"Fine, thanks." She laced her fingers in her lap again and trembled inside. What now? What should she say?

"We saw your car outside," Mrs. Sullivan said, turning to her son. "We've been out to dinner. We thought we'd stop in and see what was keeping you here after hours."

Kelly's face burned. She felt her smile quiver, then fall away.

"I decided to show Kelly my office," Beau said, having regained his equilibrium. He sat down right next to Kelly and actually draped his arm about her shoulders. "We were just discussing where we might eat dinner. Got any suggestions?"

"We ate at Hamburger Heaven. It's always good and not expensive," Mr. Sullivan said. "Of course, you two might want to go someplace fancy."

"A hamburger sounds good, doesn't it?" Beau asked, squeezing her shoulder and making her respond.

"Yes," she lied, knowing she couldn't eat a bite.

"Well, we'll be on our way." Mrs. Sullivan stood back and gave her son and former daughter-in-law a thorough once-over that ended in a sigh and a smile. "It is good to see you again, Kelly. You look—well, you look simply wonderful."

"Thank you." Kelly managed to smile back at the kind woman.

Mr. Sullivan started toward the door, then stopped and looked down at something on the carpet. Kelly followed his eye line and felt the color drain from her face when she saw one of her ivory hair combs near the toe of Mr. Sullivan's shoe. She touched the place where the comb had been before Beau's restless hands had dislodged it.

"Let me get that, Dad," Beau said, lifting his arm from Kelly's shoulder to pick up the comb and hand it to her. Without any further regard to the telltale sign, Beau walked his parents to the door. "I'll see you guys in a few days."

"All right," Mrs. Sullivan said, bussing his cheek. "Good night, hon."

"'Night, Mom. 'Night, Dad." He winked at them and closed the door, then turned and leaned back against it. He was smiling. "I wish I had a camera to capture the look on your face."

Kelly covered her look with her hands. "What must they think?"

"They're not stupid, Kelly. They think we were making out on the couch and they interrupted us."

She replaced the comb in her hair with shaking fingers. "I've never been so mortified in my life! When your dad saw my comb on the floor, I just died!"

"Oh, stop it," he scolded gently, taking one of her hands and pulling her up to her feet. "No need to be so melodramatic."

"No need? Beau, they caught us red-handed!"

"So what? Sooner or later, they would have caught on. I'm not hiding my feelings for you—from anyone." He examined her flushed face and rolled his eyes. "Oh, come on. Let's get out of here. I can tell that I won't be getting you back on the couch." He grabbed his keys and the door locked behind them.

They left the office building without another word to each other. The drive back to Beau's was just as quietly uncomfortable. Kelly stared out the window, telling herself that Beau was right but still feeling as if she'd been caught. Caught? At what? She was still angry and confused when Beau stopped the car in front of his home.

"Come inside," he said, getting out of the car. "I want to discuss something with you."

Kelly went with him into the motor home, wanting to clear things up but not sure how she'd manage it. She settled herself on the couch, and Beau sat beside her, slanting one knee across the cushions as he turned sideways to face her. The last, weak bands of sunlight fell across his face, creating a pattern of shadow and light that made Kelly want to trace it with her fingertips.

"I've been thinking about the problem at the mall," he said, resting one elbow on the back of the couch and leaning his temple against his fist. Her sharp sigh narrowed his eyes. "What's wrong?"

"I thought we were going to discuss us."

"We will. Later. I'm giving you a chance to collect yourself."

She smiled and nodded. "Good move. Go ahead. What about the mall?"

Concentration pinched the skin between his eyes. "I've got to corner this guy...or gal. Like I said before, the mall executives are leaning on me for results. Most of the stores have had employee lockers installed, which has spoiled the thief's fun. The last victims were at stores without employee lockers. All I've done so far is shrink his territory."

"That's something, at least. We haven't had any problems recently."

"Yes, but I haven't caught the thief. I want to catch him. I can do that, I think, if you'll help me."

"How can I help?"

"I'm going to leave a purse in the locker room as a decoy. Inside, among other things, will be a credit card that will have a tracer on it. When it's used to make a purchase, it will emit a signal, alerting the sales clerk, who'll call me, and I'll make the arrest. Simple, huh?"

"Sounds that way," she said, but she wondered if it was *that* simple.

"What I need is a woman's purse. Just a loan. I'll give it back in a couple of days."

"You want me to give you one of my purses?"

"Yes, and put some stuff inside it. Make it look real. An old wallet, keys, perfume—whatever women carry. But, above all else, just a little money—no more than a dollar or two—and no credit cards. We don't want to give him a choice. My card will be the only one in the purse. Bring it with you to work tomorrow. I'll pick it up from you and set the trap in the break room. Got it?"

"I guess so." She thought for a few moments, going over the plan slowly and carefully. "But what if one of my employees brings the purse to my office? I mean, it will look funny just lying around when everyone's got lockers."

"Not necessarily, but if that happens, thank the person and call me. I'll put the purse back in the break room when the coast is clear. Let's hope my plan works."

"Believe me, I do. When the thief is caught, it'll be one less worry for me."

"Is Cauley putting pressure on you because your department was picked on for a while?"

"Yes. I mean no." She shook her head.

"Which is it?" he asked, and he dropped his hand to her shoulder, pressing it lightly.

"I...I..." She sighed fretfully as he gently massaged her neck muscles. Kelly sat forward, away from his kneading fingers. "I can't think when you do that," she admitted, then gathered her thoughts. "Mr. Cauley isn't putting on the pressure. I am. I have a tendency to take responsibility for everything. It's a holdover from my former self. Bette's forever telling me to lighten up and not take the weight of the world on my shoulders."

"Bette's right. The muscles in your shoulders and neck are all bunched up. You're too tense."

"That's the way I'm made. I have this wild idea that all troubles can be tracked back to me."

"A true daughter of Eve," he joked, then sat forward and placed his hands upon her shoulders again. "Don't pull away from me," he said in a gruff whisper. His thumbs made lazy, persuasive circles on either side of her backbone. "That's better," he said after a minute. "Kelly, if the credit-card thief is anybody's fault, he's mine. I was hired to stop him."

"What will you do once he's caught?"

"Move on, I suppose."

"Move on." She closed her eyes, thinking that Beau hadn't changed all that much. He might dream of domestic bliss, but he talked like a traveling man. "I guess I should take your cue and get moving myself."

"That wasn't meant to be a cue." His hands remained solidly on her shoulders, keeping her on the couch and not letting her move away from him. "Don't go, Kelly."

"I really should—"

"Don't." He kissed the side of her neck. "Last time I was your indulgence, so how about you indulging me this time?"

She twisted around to face him and saw the lingering pain in his eyes. "You're not an indulgence, Beau. You weren't then, and you're not now. I was nervous, and I said some things I didn't mean. Please believe me."

He smiled and dropped a cool kiss upon her lips. "When you look at me like that, I'd believe that night was day." He leaned back to regard her with unnerving intensity. "You know, I think you not only take responsibility for things that aren't your fault, but you might even take the blame for things that haven't even happened yet."

"What do you mean?"

"You worry about what people will think about us being lovers before we're even there yet. One night does not lovers make."

"Oh, no?" she asked, catching the slight teasing quality in his voice.

"No," he assured her. "Usually it takes two nights."

"I see." She paused a few seconds and knew he was holding his breath. "Want to make it official?"

He released his breath in a sinking moan. "I thought you'd never ask."

Nine

"What am I doing?" Kelly asked, laughing nervously as she sprang from the couch. She faced Beau with a mixture of chagrin and temptation. "I came over here to thank you for intervening with Ryan."

"You did that. Mission accomplished." Beau reached out and grasped her hands. "Now, come back here."

"And I was going to use what happened this afternoon as an illustration of the kind of sticky situation we'll find ourselves in again and again if we don't stop seeing each other!" She pressed her hands to the sides of her head in a moment of total frustration. "What's wrong with me?"

"Nothing."

"Something's wrong. I'm not usually so—" She gulped down the rest of the sentence as Beau rose slowly from the couch and stepped right up to her. He brought his hands to her shoulders and angled her chin up with his thumbs. "Beau, we really shouldn't...."

"That's not what your eyes are saying right now."
"Oh?"
"Those lovely blue eyes of yours are begging me to kiss you."

She closed her eyes, and he laughed low in his throat. His mouth covered hers and tugged gently with small, smacking sounds that made her smile.

"Quit worrying about things you can't change," he whispered against her lips.

"But can't you see how complicated things are getting?" She opened her eyes to see his lopsided grin. "I mean it!"

"We're a curiosity now, but we'll be yesterday's news within a few weeks."

"You think so?"

"I know it. It's human nature." He nudged her nose with his and brought his hands up to frame her face. "At first our families and friends might look askance at us, but then we'll become old hat to them, and they'll move on to the next curiosity."

"I hope you're right. I don't like being a curiosity."

He chuckled warmly, then grasped her hands and began walking backward to his bedroom, pulling Kelly along. "Let me romance you, Kelly," he urged in an enticing whisper. "You don't even have to take responsibility or blame for us. I'll be glad to shoulder it all for the pure pleasure of having you."

Emotion caught in her throat. Never had a man spoken so eloquently to her! How could she resist a man with a smile that took years off him and her, with eyes that shone with confidence in both himself and in her? Simple. She couldn't resist!

She ran two short steps into his arms, her eyes filling with sentimental tears and her trembling lower lip caught between her teeth. She linked her hands around his neck, rising up on tiptoe as his arms wound around her waist.

She gave her lips to him, loving the lush, openmouthed kisses he placed upon them. Her lips were moist and trembling when his mouth lifted away, and she saw that his mouth was slick from her kisses. She didn't need to see that he was aroused. She could feel it. His body was as taut and quivering as a plucked violin string.

He reached back blindly and closed the door, shutting them away from the rest of the world, then he kicked off his shoes and began unbuttoning the gauze shirt. Kelly trusted her instincts and deftly moved aside his hands. She unbuttoned the next ivory disc, halfway down his chest, then separated the fabric and pressed her lips to the skin she exposed. She inched her hands inside the shirt and around to his ribs where his skin was more sensitive to her touch. He trembled beneath her stroking fingertips. She pressed her mouth to one of his flat nipples and felt an immediate quickening within him.

Responding to her minute ministrations, Beau yanked the shirt free of his belt and let the tails hang, limp and wrinkled.

He felt a little that way himself—strangely without form or shape—as Kelly continued her exploration. Her fingers were cool upon his heated flesh, and her mouth was a tiny suction on strategic patches of his skin. When she closed her lips around one of his dark paps again, he thought he might die of pleasure. He groaned as a sweet aching overtook him. He took her by the elbows and moved her backward to the bed, shivering and trembling as he did so, amazed by the sheer power she could exercise over him. He wanted her so intensely that it scared him at times—at times like this, especially, when she was so eager to please him and to be pleased by him.

Kelly sat on the bed for a few moments, taking her cues from him. But he made no further move. He stared at her with a sort of wonder, even awe. She kicked off her sandals and pulled her chocolate-striped shirt free of the waistband of her brown trousers. She unbuttoned the shirt and let it slip from her arms, then she tossed it aside. Beau made no move toward her, but she noticed that his breathing had grown short and choppy. She reached around to unfasten her bra, and Beau fell to his knees before her. He discarded the frilly strip with a wild fling, then buried his face between her breasts. His actions were so swift, so sure, that Kelly could only let it happen. Her head fell back and then her body followed. The coverlet beneath her was a blue quilted satin. It whispered to her with each movement she made.

Beau showered her breasts and stomach with tiny kisses that made her tremble. He pulled her trousers down her slim, shapely legs, then dispensed with the final, lacy barrier. He gripped her wrists and pulled her up off the bed and into his arms. She laughed, surprised at first, then she nodded in agreement when he yanked the coverlet off the bed and let it pool on the floor.

Kelly went to the head of the bed and turned down the lime-green sheet. She kept her gaze averted, but she knew that Beau was removing the rest of his clothing. She couldn't recall much about his body in her dreams. The other time, she'd been so wrapped up in the experience of making love to a man who wasn't her husband that it was all she could do to keep her misgivings at bay and enjoy the newness of it all.

There were no misgivings to fight this time, leaving her mind free of obstacles. The room was in twilight and limned with smoky mauve. Beau stretched out on the bed, crossing his ankles, and lacing his fingers behind his head. Kelly stared at a point just to the left of his lean body.

"Kelly?" He extended a hand to her. "Come here, honey."

She smiled, and her heart filled with a wondrous thing. Love, she thought, and her smile took on a different tilt. She was in love again. She let him take her hand, but she held back a few moments to look upon the man who had proven to her that loving could be better, stronger, more appreciated, the second time around.

He was so still that he could have been a statue that had fallen across the bed. Bronze, powerfully sculpted, a study in male repose, he was an inspiration for an artist's eye. Most of his body was covered with crisp, auburn hair tipped with gold. Power flexed under his skin, toughened to a leathery texture. Shadow and darker shadow created hills and valleys, concealing some things and revealing others. Kelly saw enough to know that he wanted her.

Impatience tightened his hold, and he pulled her across him. He was warm and solid. Everything a man should be, she thought. His soft caresses communicated his fiery desire. Each kiss seemed to increase his ardor. Kelly sat astride him, no longer guarded by her own shyness. She positioned herself over him and then descended slowly until she was full of him. His hips bucked beneath her, but she kept control of the union and set a honeyed, unhurried pace. She closed her eyes, then squeezed them shut so tightly that tears pooled in their corners. The world ceased to exist for her. Only the joining of her body with his was given any credence. Perspiration ran in tiny rivulets down her sides where he held her. Small sounds of passion bubbled past her lips, then her throat constricted as her pleasure increased until she cried out. The world became a shooting star with her in its center.

She was limp with exultation, and hardly aware of being flipped onto her back. Only when Beau entered her again from his new vantage point did she open her eyes to take in the virile beauty in the planes of his face and in the limpid green passion of his eyes.

His final thrust lifted her hips from the bed. Kelly clung to him, bringing his head down to her breasts where her heart was singing.

"I love you," she said. So natural. So wonderful.

"I know," he replied, then raised his head to share with her his smile of jubilation.

Kelly buzzed around her house, plumping pillows, arranging flowers, fanning magazines on the end tables and humming happily to herself.

She glanced at the clock and smiled when she saw that it was only a few minutes before seven. Beau would be ringing her doorbell any minute. The time was finally at hand. During work that day she couldn't concentrate on anything for more than a few minutes at a time. She'd brought the purse and contents for Beau's trap. The sight of him and her brief visit with him that day had created a glow within her and stirred memories of last night.

Kelly pirouetted in the center of her living room, then laughed at herself. She was in love! Giddy with it, obsessed with it, all aglow with it! Oh, what a wonderful feeling, she thought. How could she have lived so long without it? She had trouble remembering how she'd felt when she'd fallen in love for the first time with that other Sullivan. But it couldn't have felt *this* good, she told herself. She'd never in her life felt *this* good about herself and life in general. Even the credit-card thief and other problems at work didn't make a dent in her rosy outlook.

When had it all happened? What was the exact moment when she knew, with clarity and certainty, that Beau was the most important person in her life? When had she stopped thinking of him as Ryan's brother and started thinking of him as the man in her life?

The chiming door bell ended her unanswered questions. She fairly flew to the door and flung it open. He stood on her porch, arms held out from his sides so that he could pose properly in his suit of clothes, which she'd helped him select. The handsome blazer, matching trousers with crisp front pleats, pale blue shirt and madras tie of navy-and-sapphire plaid were a perfect combination. His dark hair, curling just a bit, had been carefully combed for the occasion, and Kelly would bet her next month's salary that he'd shaved no more than ten minutes ago. The aroma of his after-shave floated to her, spicy and manly.

Kelly smiled her approval, then reached out to grab the sides of his jacket and pull him into her house and her arms. She kissed him with the confidence of a woman rightly loved.

"I missed you," she confessed in a voice husky with emotion. "I've had such a lovely day. I've spent it thinking of you, when I should have concentrated on the sales receipts from our Labor Day campaign."

"I like you in this mood," he said, dropping a kiss upon her lips. "You've been on my mind, too. I feel like a new man, and I know I look like one."

"You looked great before I got hold of you." She stood back for a more thorough scrutiny. "I wish I could take the credit, but my contribution has been minimal. You look fabulous, Beau Sullivan."

"You look scrumptious yourself," he said, taking her hands and holding them out from her sides so that he could fully appreciate her carefully chosen short, white pleated skirt, which showed off her firm, tanned legs, and golden-yellow sleeveless blouse of jersey knit. She'd left her ebony hair free and flowing.

"Would you like something to drink?"

"No, let's go."

"Where are you taking me?" she asked, tucking her purse under one arm, then locking the front door behind her.

"To a place where I can show you off," he said, winking. "You'll find out when we get there."

"I love a man of mystery." She sat in the passenger's seat and waited for him to settle behind the steering wheel. "Speaking of mysteries, I guess you like them or you wouldn't be a detective."

"I guess you're right," he said, settling more comfortably in the driver's seat and hooking a wrist over the wheel as the car purred along the street.

"Tell me about your work," she said. "Which job did you enjoy the most?"

"The one I'm doing now. My dream for several years has been to open my own agency so that I could do things my own way. This happens to be the best time of my life."

"Is it?" Happiness welled inside her. She was part of the best time of his life, she told herself, feeling giddy and young and wonderfully alive. "But what about all those exotic places you've visited? Don't you miss seeing the wonders of the world?"

"Let me tell you something about the wonders of the world," he said, glancing her way. "They're not so wonderful when you're alone. I've seen the Great Pyramids, the Parthenon, Easter Island, the Sahara, the Grand Canyon and Old Faithful, but they weren't all that exciting at the time. I held it all inside because there was no one special there to share the wonder of it all with me. That's when you know the difference from being alone and being lonely. I've been lonely too often the last few years."

"A man as good-looking as you didn't have to be lonely," Kelly said.

"No, but sometimes finding a soul mate is about as easy as finding a needle in a haystack."

"You're so different from the way I had you figured," she confessed, staring off into the distance where tall grasses swayed and the ocean reigned supreme. "My impressions of you were of a man happy with his solitary life. I imagined that you were an American James Bond."

He laughed at that, shaking his head slowly. "James Bond, huh? Well, I certainly never thought of myself in those terms. Don't get me wrong," he said, his green eyes containing a serious glint. "I chose the life. Nobody forced me to move from one place to the other, from one job to the next. I did it because that's what I thought I needed. I'm from a big family, and I was sick of sharing everything. I wanted my own room and my own things. But you can have too much of a good thing. A couple of years ago it occurred to me that I was moving around a lot because I was unhappy. What do you do when your life gets boring, unpleasant or unsettling?"

"Move on," Kelly said mostly to herself. She remembered him saying that only yesterday. What would he do when his life in St. Augustine failed to hold his interest? Move on. He'd said it himself. That's the way he was made.

"That's right," he agreed. "Move on. I keep moving because I'm searching for something, but I just can't seem to find it. My family says I'm looking for *someone*, not something."

"Maybe you don't need anyone. There's nothing wrong with being self-sufficient, you know."

"Yes, I know," he conceded with a frown. "But humans are social creatures. We travel in packs. Families, if you will. It's been an eye-opener for me to hear of your struggle for an independent life. I've been an independent operator for so long that I never gave it much thought. But take it from a maverick; there's a happy middle ground to everything. Being your own person and depending only on yourself is fine up to a point."

"I don't know...." She examined her own feelings and experiences before she went on. "I don't want to surrender my freedom again. Not even for love."

"Loving someone doesn't have to be a surrender. It can be a victory." He steered the car into a packed parking lot. "Surprise!"

Kelly smiled, realizing that he'd brought her to an outdoor concert. "I read about this in the newspaper. I love big-band music. How did you know?"

"I didn't. Just went with my instincts."

"Good instincts."

He parked the car and switched off the motor, then turned sideways to face her. He took one of her hands in his, smiling in a way that made her feel warm inside. The setting sun outlined them in gold. The music, full-bodied and lush, floated to them. Although they were surrounded by others, intimacy quivered in the air.

"Did you trap a thief today?" Kelly asked.

"No, but I'm going to give it a few more days." He lifted her hand and placed a kiss in her palm. His gaze was inescapable. "Have you told your parents that you're involved with another Sullivan?"

"No, not yet. But I will."

"It's up to you." He shrugged nonchalantly. "I don't think they'll have any strong objections."

"No, I don't think so either. I'm a grown woman, after all, and can see whomever I like."

"So why haven't you told your parents?"

"I haven't talked to them lately," she countered with a saucy smile. "I tried to phone them a couple of times, but they must be on a trip or something. Dad still plays golf, and Mother travels with him sometimes."

"He still plays professionally?"

"No, but he's semipro now. He plays in the senior citizens' tournaments. He's been in a couple of the Grand Masters events, too."

"Good for him. People should stay active as long as possible. Do you play?"

"No." She laughed, thinking of her father's exasperation when she'd shown no interest in sports whatsoever. "I'm my mother's daughter on that score. Mother and I make good spectators."

She couldn't quite decipher his mood. He was contemplative and unusually quiet. "Beau, are you discouraged that your trap didn't work?"

"No, not really. Maybe he wasn't at the mall today, or maybe he didn't see the purse. I'll give a few days before I worry about it. I think he'll bite when the time is right. Oh, I almost forgot! I got another job today."

"Really? Doing what?"

"I was hired to find my client's accountant, who took a powder a couple of weeks ago. He also took my client's investment money with him."

"Uh-oh."

"Yes, that's a big uh-oh. I did some preliminary work this afternoon, and I've got a good idea that the guy might be staying with his lady friend in New York City. I've got a policeman friend there checking it out for me."

"I bet you've got valuable friends all over the place, don't you?"

"It helps to know the right people," he conceded. "If my hunch pays off, I'll fly to Manhattan in a few days for a personal visit. It'll be great to be in New York again. I've got lots of old friends there. It's a wonderful city. Autumn in New York." He paused to savor a picture in his mind. "That's one thing I don't like about Florida. No seasons. I miss autumn and winter."

"You won't go to see the accountant alone, will you? I mean, that could be dangerous. He might pull a gun or put up a fight or something like that!"

"I can handle myself." The tone of his voice and the set of his jaw spoke of a steely disposition and a will of iron.

"I've noticed. I wouldn't mind putting my life in your hands if I felt endangered."

"Thanks. I needed that." He looked in the direction of the music. "Shall we go?"

The night was soft and breezy, perfect for a concert under the stars. The moon, a milky disc, beamed down a soft spotlight. The orchestra sent out the sweet, familiar notes of an Irving Berlin classic. Half of the crowd was seated in the bleachers, and the other half was in the dance area in front of the orchestra platform, moving two by two, cheek to cheek. Kelly and Beau joined them. They held each other close, his arms around her waist and hers draped over his shoulders.

A singer with a smoky alto made for seduction came to the mike to croon some smooth songs from the forties and early fifties. Beau and Kelly never entertained the thought of sitting any of them out.

"This was a great idea," Kelly said, sighing when Beau kissed her temple and then her cheek.

She tipped back her head to smile at him, then closed her eyes when his mouth swept across hers in a sliding, satiny kiss. The man had an inexhaustible repertoire of kisses, Kelly thought, and she was more than happy to let him practice them on her. He was tall and her arms began to ache, so she moved them from his broad shoulders to the crooks of his arms and laid her cheek against his shirtfront as the music played on and on.

When the orchestra took a break, Beau took Kelly's hand and led her toward a refreshment stand. He bought raspberry snow cones and found an unoccupied bench near the water. The breeze off the ocean was salty and warm for autumn. It fluttered the hem of Kelly's pleated skirt and blew her hair back from her face.

They munched on their snow cones and watched the others around them. The people were of all ages, from teens to senior citizens. Couples surrounded them, and Kelly was reminded of what Beau had said to her once about being alone on holidays.

"I never gave it much thought until lately, but ours is a society of pairs, isn't it?" Kelly swept an arm before her. "Look around. What do you see? Couples. I can remember seeing only one single man all the time we've been here, and I felt sorry for him. He seemed so pitiful, wandering around with no one at his side."

"Like me."

"I'm with you," Kelly reminded him, taking one of his hands in hers.

"Yes, but before there was you, there was me, all alone. You never felt lonely after your divorce?"

"Not often. But I've good friends like Bette. Don't you?"

"No, not consistent ones. Acquaintances is a better word. I think women bond with women much easier than men bond with men. Men know each other through activities like sports or hobbies. Women don't need excuses to make friends. They don't have fishing buddies, tennis friends, women they see only during bridge games."

"You may be right," she said, thinking that Beau was opening all kinds of thoughtful avenues for her. He'd given so many things deep thought that it occurred to her that he was most probably an introvert, while she was an extrovert.

"Women are more loyal in their friendships. For instance, men go to clubs with their buddies, but if one of the guys manages to interest a woman, then off he goes without a thought to the buddies he's leaving behind. But I've seen women in the very same situation refuse to go off with a guy because they wouldn't leave their friends. I've had that happen to me several times. Usually, the lady gives me her telephone number and asks me to call her sometime, but she won't leave her friends in the lurch."

"Do you approve or disapprove?" Kelly asked.

"I think it's marvelous!" His smile was one of delight. "Men could learn from the way women guard their friendships. After all, one can learn loyalty and integrity by being someone's best friend. But I know men who've never really had a *best* friend. Know why?"

"Because you have to be one before you can have one," Kelly said, winning a quick kiss from him, his snow-cone-cold lips pressing hard upon her warm forehead.

"That's right! You're as smart as you are beautiful. What a powerful combination." He put one arm around her and hugged her to his side. "You and the night and the music. I think I'm in big trouble."

"Don't worry," she said, laughing at his feigned shudder. "I think you can handle us."

She looked into his eyes, and he into hers. Wordlessly, they rose from the bench and didn't return to the dance floor. Instead, they went to Beau's car and he drove them back to Kelly's house.

Kelly closed and locked the front door, then was spun around to receive Beau's kiss of fire. The moment she'd waited for all day and most of the evening was finally hers, and Kelly wasted no more precious time. She pushed off his jacket and let it fall, unheeded, to the floor. Then she loosened his tie with hasty, almost rough jerks, until she could toss it aside, followed swiftly by his shirt. She ran her hands over his shoulders, down his arms, across the palms of his hands. Then repeated the journey, this time detouring at his elbows to stroke his ribs and back. He moaned deep in his throat.

"Kelly, let me...."

His unfinished request needed no translation. She stood still long enough for him to pull the blouse over her head, then smooth her hair back from her face. His movements were hurried but not rough as he flung aside her bra, then helped her out of the rest of her clothes. She went to the bedroom, motioning for him to hurry, then laughing when he almost fell while trying to walk and remove his trousers at the same time.

Finally, they were together on Kelly's bed of white linen, their bodies surging together in a quest for a fulfillment they had come to crave.

Beau was delighted and surprised by Kelly's forceful lovemaking on this night. Before, she'd been receptive, giving, even enthusiastic, but always with an underlining modesty that bordered on hesitancy. Tonight, however, she was a different woman. She took as much as she gave, she demanded more of him than ever before, and she pushed him to an awakening of his own prowess. In short, it took everything he had to keep up with her.

She was all fire and brimstone, writhing beneath him, caressing him with hands that stoked and banked his passion whispering encouragingly and sometimes impatiently in his ear. Her zenith set her off like a Roman candle, and Beau could only hold on until she floated back to him as gentle as a leaf on the wind.

"Easy," he whispered, smoothing the hair back from her damp forehead and temples. "Let's take it slow this time, hmmm?" He kissed her lips, relaxed and undemanding beneath his. Her hands rested placidly upon his hips. He couldn't make up his mind whether he liked her better as the firebrand she'd been a few moments ago or as the fragile flower he now held in his arms.

He felt like the lucky prince kissing Snow White back into the world of the living, the world of the loving. Gradually Kelly roused from her time of repose. Her mouth clung to his, then she began kissing him back. Her tongue parried, teased, explored. Her hands moved to his waist. Her knees came up to cradle his hips. He traveled down her lithe body, tracing its curves, its dips, its risings, with his lips. He touched her secret places with the tip of his tongue. He memorized her beauty with his hands and his eyes. He nuzzled her inner thighs, then the backs of her knees, where the skin was so soft, so delicate.

Lacing his fingers in hers, he glided up her body and pressed her hands into the pillow on either side of her head. Then he joined his body with hers again, slower this time and with more care, because he knew she'd be tender and trembling from their other full embrace. Linked to her, he felt as if he could solve the puzzles of the world. He knew what inspired artists, writers, musicians and scientists. He understood the "calling" of some men by a higher being. He empathized with those who weren't satisfied with this world but wanted to stretch the boundaries of outer space. He felt the force that drove men to build pyramids and monuments and monoliths. If one woman could make him know and feel and believe all of this, then surely nothing was impossible!

He took one of her rosy nipples in his mouth and felt her heart leaping against his lips. And then his own heart seemed to explode and pour into her. He lost himself and became one with her. Lights flashed behind his eyelids as he lifted his head and gasped for breath. Kelly hugged him with arms and legs. Her voice floated to him like an autumn wind, flowing through his mind and cooling his body.

Beau kissed her, then sucked gently on her lower lip until she smiled. "I love you," he said.

"I know," she said, still smiling.

It was raining Monday morning, but it didn't dampen Kelly's spirits. She arrived at work a half hour before schedule, walked briskly through her department, unconsciously checking displays and access aisles.

For the past six nights, she'd been with Beau. Sometimes her place, sometimes his, always together. He'd risen early that morning and was gone by the time she was awakened by his alarm. She vaguely remembered hearing the telephone ring. Beau had answered it, or had that been a dream?

She'd showered and dressed, then stopped by her place on the way to work for a quick breakfast of coffee and croissants and to read the morning newspaper. Keeping up with current events was her only lifeline to that other world out there, the one that didn't revolve around Beau Sullivan.

Through him, she'd remembered the good things about being a couple. She'd also realized that since her divorce she'd dwelled on the bad side of twosomes. But Beau had made her familiar once again with the little pleasures of cooking together, eating together, shopping together, cuddling in front of the television together, and just talking for hours and hours. The best thing about Beau was that he let her have her own set of values, ideas and preferences even though he might not share them. He listened to her views of politics, theater, books, even the best way to prepare swordfish, then shared his differing point of view without making it seem as if he were right and she were dead wrong.

For that alone, she loved him dearly. There were so many reasons for loving him that it simply boggled her mind!

She swung around the corner of her office and was inside it before she noticed the two men sitting in front of her desk. Both rose to their feet, gaunt faced and foreboding. Kelly looked from Beau to Joe Cauley, wondering what bad news they carried.

"Good morning," she said, mainly addressing Beau, but he didn't return her smile. She looked at Cauley. He was perspiring freely, his face beet red. "What's going on, Mr. Cauley? Did the credit-card thief strike again?"

"Yes, he did," Cauley said, then sat heavily in the chair. "He hit your department again."

Kelly looked at Beau, only then realizing that the news was both good and bad. "You caught him?"

"That's right," Beau said, then motioned toward the chair behind her desk. "Have a seat."

THE SECOND MR. SULLIVAN

Beau helped her out of her raincoat, and she hung it away along with her umbrella, then she sat down and waited for Beau to drop the other shoe.

"Remember Julie Scott?" he asked.

"Not Julie! I haven't seen her around since I let her go." Kelly realized that she was halfway out of her chair. She sat down and cautioned herself to stay calm. Don't get defensive, she told herself firmly. None of this is your fault, and nobody's asking you to take the blame or make excuses for yourself or anybody else!

"Not Julie," Mr. Cauley spoke up. "Julie's boyfriend."

"Her boyfriend?" Kelly shook her head. "I don't know him."

"Tommy Holder," Beau supplied, consulting a sheet of paper in his hands. "Eighteen years old, works part-time in—"

"Electronics department," Kelly finished with a nod. "Yes, I've seen him around, but I didn't know that he was Julie's boyfriend."

"Well, from what I've gathered, Julie is more serious about him than he is about her. He went with her as long as it was convenient for him. She told him the layout of this department and the one she used to work in...." He paused to consult his notes.

"Cosmetics," Kelly said.

"That's right. Cosmetics. After Julie got fired and Tommy didn't see her so often, the romance cooled."

"Tommy took the prop purse?" she asked.

"Yes. He tried to charge an electric keyboard with the card last night. The store manager called early this morning."

"Oh, right." She nodded, remembering the phone call more clearly. "And the store was in this mall?"

"Music Plus," Mr. Cauley said. He was slumped in his chair, and Kelly couldn't tell if he was exhausted now that it was over, or if he was disappointed that the chase was finished. "The police have been called in on this, but they don't think the merchandise will be recovered."

"I imagine Tommy's pawned or sold it all by now," Beau said. "At the most, he might have kept one or two things for his own use."

"So, he was taking the cards, charging things on them, then putting them back before anyone missed them," Kelly said, going over it for herself as much as for anyone else.

"That's the scam," Beau said, giving her a grin that lifted her trodden spirits. "But that scam is history now. Tommy's downtown singing the blues."

Despite the gravity of the situation, Kelly couldn't help but laugh under her breath at Beau's private-eye talk. She sensed that he was relieved to see the end of the credit-card caper. The end.

The finality triggered apprehension in Kelly. Her memory played Beau's voice over and over again in her head saying, "Move on. Move on. Move on." Traveling man. That was Beau. Wasn't it? Was she foolish to think that she'd changed him into a homebody?

"Mr. Cauley, we owe a debt of gratitude to Ms. Sullivan for her assistance in apprehending the suspect," Beau said, suddenly grave and all business.

"How's that?" Cauley asked, pushing up from his chair like a sleeper surfacing from a bad dream.

"She helped me execute the plan that ultimately smoked out Tommy Holder."

"Is that so!" Cauley turned to Kelly, his hand extended. "Good job, Kelly. I'll be sure and mention this to the Wysart executives."

"I only did what anyone else would do," Kelly said, accepting Cauley's handshake but feeling strange about accepting Beau's glowing report on her part in setting the trap. "I really didn't do that much."

"Well, you did something, and that's more than we can say about any other store manager," Beau said. "Right, Mr. Cauley? I think she deserves some recognition. Not every employee takes an active part in the apprehension of criminals."

"Beau, please!" Kelly laughed and sent him a chiding glance. "He's exaggerating, Mr. Cauley."

"Kelly Sullivan, you should take credit when credit's due," Cauley said, giving her a stern glare. "That's the only way to climb up the ladder of success. Humility is seldom rewarded in retail. I'm going to include your good deed in my report on this matter." He turned to Beau and shook his hand. "I'm certainly glad to see this cleared up, Sullivan. If you'll come to my office, we'll file a final report."

"Give me just a few minutes, and I'll be right with you."

"Okay." Mr. Cauley waved briefly in Kelly's direction as he hustled out of the office. "Have a good day."

"Yes, sir. I'll do that," Kelly called after him. "I guess you're proud of yourself, Beau Sullivan." She arched a brow, her gaze sweeping from his dark red hair to the toes of his tennis shoes. He'd dressed casually today in jeans and a pullover shirt of emerald green.

"Shouldn't I be?"

"Yes, but you lathered it on pretty thick about my part in this. You didn't have to do that."

"I wanted to do it. I know how much you wanted the thief caught. Well, we've got him. Case closed."

"Case closed." The finality struck her another blow, and she knew that if she'd been standing, her knees would have buckled. "What now?"

"I've got to meet with Cauley as promised. What time are you getting off work tonight?"

"Five or six."

"Your place or mine, at seven?"

"I..." She hesitated, her mind in a whirl, her heart sinking even though she knew it shouldn't be. But she kept thinking about Tommy and Julie. Their romance had ended when Julie no longer saw Tommy at work every day. Sure, it was a teenage romance, but it happened with adults' romances, too. Passion died fast sometimes. It didn't always last long enough to mellow into a deep and abiding love.

"Kelly? Do you read me?" Beau asked, leaning into her face. "Your place or mine?"

"I'll let you know later, okay?"

"Should I call you?"

"Yes. Call." She smiled, but she knew by the flash of concern in his eyes that her smile was weak and uncertain.

"Are you okay?" he asked.

"Yes. I'm fine," she lied.

"Okay," he said dubiously. He straightened and headed for the doorway. "I'm gone, Kelly."

Gone?

"Beau!" She shot up from the chair and extended one hand before she realized what she was doing.

"What, honey?" He brought his brows together in a frown.

"Nothing." She laughed, shooing him with her hands. "Go on to your meeting. It'll keep until tonight."

"Are you sure?"

"Yes." She blew him a kiss, which he caught and tucked into the pocket of his shirt.

Ten

It was nearly eight o'clock before Beau's black Corvette pulled into Kelly's driveway. Kelly watched him from the front window. He bounded from the car, still dressed in the jeans and pullover he'd been wearing that morning, and came to the porch at a lope. Kelly had rushed home from work, taken a shower, washed and styled her hair, put on a clean, fresh sundress of cranberry seersucker and repaired her makeup. She felt a compulsion to look her best for him. In fact, she thought, compulsion wasn't quite the word. Desperation was more accurate. She shuddered.

What was wrong with her? So the credit-card thief had been caught and the case was closed. That didn't mean Beau would hit the road, and if he did, she'd get along just fine. She wouldn't be a clinging vine. She wouldn't beg him to stay. Tipping up her chin at a determined angle, Kelly opened the door before he could ring the bell.

"Sorry I'm late. I connected with that friend of mine in New York. He called long-distance just as I was going out the door." Beau came inside and sprawled in the nearest chair. "My hunch paid off, so I'm going to New York day after tomorrow."

"I see." Kelly noted the sparkle of excitement in his eyes. He had the look of a man who'd been sprung from prison. "Have you had dinner?"

"No, but don't trouble yourself."

"No trouble. I've been waiting for you," she said, placing the sting of a whip in her words. "Lucky for both of us I prepared a shrimp salad and it could be held until you showed up."

"Kelly, I said I was sorry."

"Beau, I heard you." She marched into the kitchen and flung open the refrigerator door. The salad looked about as appetizing to her as a boiled shoe.

"What can I do to help?"

"Put this on the table," she said, reaching in for the salad and handing it to him. "I'll put ice in the glasses. The table is set."

"Say, this looks great."

"It looked better at six-thirty."

"All right, damn it!"

Kelly snapped to attention, realizing that she'd never really seen him angry until now. He was furious! Red-faced, clenched fists, jaw muscles flexing. She was transfixed, astounded by his flash of Irish temper.

"I'm an hour and a half late, and I'm sorry. What more do you want, Kelly?" he asked, head thrust forward like a raging bull.

Kelly joined him in the dining room and poured the tea into the glasses of ice, giving herself time to think. "Maybe we've been seeing too much of each other. It's true that I'm put out with you for making me hold dinner, but that's because I'm used to eating on my own schedule. I like eating when *I* want to and not having to wait for somebody else. We're both set in our ways, and we're probably getting on each other's nerves."

He waited for her to sit at the table, then he sat opposite her. "Kelly, are we going to break up because I'm late for dinner?" His tone was softer, his anger reined in for the moment. Humor had returned to his green eyes. "Look, we've been busy today and we're tired. That's all there is to it."

"I guess the mall execu—no, wait. The mall 'suits' are glad to put the thief business behind them, aren't they?"

He chuckled at her police jargon. "And how. So was I. It was my first case in St. Augustine, and I'm happy to move on to the next job."

"Moving on," Kelly said under her breath. "So, you'll be leaving for New York in a couple of days?"

"Right." He winked and made a clicking noise at the side of his mouth. "Good old New York. Can hardly wait."

"I'll bet."

"Have you ever been there?" he asked.

"As a matter of fact, I have. My parents took me there when I was seventeen. It was my last vacation with them. I was married a year later."

"Did you like New York?"

She shrugged and wrinkled her nose in distaste. "It was all right, I guess."

"Such enthusiasm!"

"So, I'm just a stick-in-the-mud," she said irritably.

"Kelly, what's wrong?" He pushed himself away from the table. "Your sense of humor has taken a turn for the worse."

"Nothing's wrong. Just because you like New York doesn't mean I have to like it. I'm not your clone. I don't want to be another man's Barbie doll!"

"Nobody's asking you to!" He stood up and raked his hands through his hair in a distracted gesture. "What's happening here? Why are you picking a fight with me?"

"I'm not." She sighed and began clearing the table. "Like I said, we've been together too much lately. Your job at the mall is over, so there's no reason for you to hang around me anymore."

"I never thought of you like that, Kelly."

"Like what?" she asked, pausing on her way to the kitchen.

"Like you were part of my work with the mall." He gathered up the rest of the dishes and followed her. "You really don't think it was part of my job to date you."

"No, but you've got to move on, and so do I."

"Are you speaking for yourself or for me?" He held up a hand before she could answer. "Because if you're speaking for me, I'd just as soon you wouldn't. Look, I think I'll go home and you can call me later. Okay?"

"Whatever." She shrugged, thinking that he'd taken the exit she'd given him. He was going, going... gone?

"Kelly?" He tipped up her chin with his hand and placed a light kiss on her lips. "If you want to talk later, call me. I think you've been under too much stress lately. Get some rest and relax, okay? You'll feel better."

"Thanks. I'll do that." She went to the front door with him. "If I don't talk to you before you go to New York, have a good time, and good luck."

He turned on the threshold. "Wait a sec." He placed three fingertips to his forehead and released a short laugh that was more incredulous than amused. "Are you telling me you're not planning on seeing me again before I go to New York? Is that what you're telling me?"

"You'll be busy," she said, shrugging. "I'll be busy."

"Kelly, you're right." He touched the side of his hand to his forehead and tossed off a salute. "You are getting on my nerves!" Then he pulled the door shut with a bang.

Kelly was a statue for several minutes, long after she heard him drive away, then she crumbled into a chair and dropped her face in her hands. She was mortified. She'd all but pushed him out the door! Maybe he hadn't been looking for an escape hatch. Maybe she'd read him all wrong.

Someone rang the doorbell, and Kelly almost flew across the room to open it, thinking that it would be Beau. But it was Bette.

"Oh, hi. Come on in." Kelly turned and dragged herself back to the easy chair. "Have a seat."

"You look nice," Bette said, glancing at her outfit, then at her face. "No, wait. You look terrible. What's going on? I couldn't believe it when I looked out and saw that you were home but Beau wasn't here. I thought you two had become inseparable."

"The bloom is off the rose, I guess." Kelly rested her head against the back cushion and sighed. "Heaven help me, I'm sounding like my mother. My dad warned me this would happen. Sit down, Bette. I need the company. Maybe you can save me from myself."

"You look like you've been run over by a truck," Bette said, sitting cross-legged on the floor in front of Kelly. She leaned back against the couch and put Kelly under an intent scrutiny. "What have you done now, Sullivan?"

Kelly laughed, thinking that Bette knew her better than she knew herself sometimes. "I wasn't very cooperative tonight. I invited Beau over for dinner, he was more than an hour late, and I just as much told him, 'Here's your hat, what's your hurry, and don't let the door hit your behind on the way out.'"

"You are sounding like your mother. But cheer up! Every great romance has its bumps." Bette angled forward and placed her hand on Kelly's arm. She gave her a little shake. "Don't lose your cool, kid. It's not the world's worst catastrophe."

"Yes, I know, but there's more."

"Oh, there's more! Do tell." Bette sat back again, arms folded, her long face set in its usual world-weary expression.

"You sure I'm not keeping you from something?" Kelly examined Bette's white shorts and blue tank top. "Were you going somewhere?"

"I'm meeting a guy down the beach later. We're going for a moonlight jog."

"Well, go! This can wait."

Bette checked her watch. "No, I've got time. Go ahead. Shoot."

Kelly lifted her arms and gripped the winged sides of the chair as she focused her thoughts on Beau. "I wish I could read his mind," she said, speaking mostly to herself.

"But you can't, so you have to ask point-blank questions. That's the mistake a lot of people make, Kelly. They beat around the bush and get nowhere fast. If you want answers, then ask questions. He can't read your mind, either. Just like this guy I'm meeting tonight. We've seen each other dozens of times on the beach, but he never would approach me. He'd just smile and jog on. Finally I stopped him the other evening and asked if he'd like to jog with me, providing he didn't have a wife waiting somewhere for him. No wife, no problem. We've been running together almost every evening this week. He says he's been wanting to talk to me for months, but he figured I wouldn't be interested." She threw up her hands. "In short, we waste a lot of time trying to second-guess other people. We've got mouths. We ought to use them for something more constructive than shoving potato chips in."

"Gosh, how'd you get so smart?" Kelly asked, only half kidding.

"It's easy to be reasonable when you're not in the eye of the storm. You're too involved to think straight."

"But what about Beau? Is he involved? Really involved? Or is he just having fun while it lasts?"

"You're asking me?" Bette widened her eyes and pointed a finger at Kelly. "You should know how he feels, and if you don't, you should ask. Provided he's important to you."

"Of course he's important!"

"Does he know that?"

"Know what? That he's important to me?" Kelly grabbed up a throw pillow and hugged it tightly as she considered the question. "I don't know. He should know. I haven't been keeping my feelings a secret."

"Maybe he thinks he's been as open as a church door on Sunday, too." Bette studied Kelly for a few moments, then shook her head. "But communication isn't your only worry, if I remember correctly. Weren't you upset because he used to be your brother-in-law?"

"Oh, that," Kelly said disparagingly.

"Yes, that. A few days ago, that was your big beef against Beau," Bette reminded her. "I guess I've missed an episode of this soap opera. Fill me in, why don't you."

"It just ceased to be important, that's all."

"Kelly Sullivan!" Bette sprang to her knees, alert and wide-eyed. "Are you in love? Have you fallen for that redheaded hunk?"

"I... well... I suppose..."

"You have!" Bette laughed, almost brayed! "This is great. And fast! He must be a go-getter. It's not your nature to fall in love with a guy in a matter of weeks, is it? You dated Ryan for three years!"

"Hold on, Bette," Kelly said, trying to rein in her friend's enthusiasm. "I'm not engaged yet. Not by a long shot. I am in love, but I'm not sure that's good or bad. Beau has never been married. He's always been an independent operator."

"But he opened an office here. Sounds permanent to me."

"He's leaving for New York in a couple of days." Kelly hugged the pillow even closer as her heart seemed to empty. "He's got friends there. He's working on a case, but I think he just wants an excuse to hit the road again. I don't think he'll be back, except to pack up his motor home and head for open spaces."

"Wait, wait, wait," Bette said, stopping her flow of speculation. "Did he say any of this, or are you attempting to read his mind again?"

"Well, he didn't say it in so many words, but I could see it in his eyes."

"The man has nice eyes," Bette agreed. "But I don't think they speak in paragraphs."

"Bette, you're a riot," Kelly said, laughing at Bette and herself. "And you're right, of course, but I've got to play some of my hunches. I figure that Beau won't be too anxious to get back here to sleepy, little St. Augustine once he's in the whirl of New York. I think it's better this way."

"What way?"

"That we end it quick and clean."

"End it?" Bette gasped, and it was the first time Kelly could remember seeing Bette exhibit extreme emotion. The usually unruffled woman jumped to her feet and began pacing in front of Kelly's chair. "Will you listen to yourself? You're throwing a good man out the window! What makes you think that you and your love can't compete with New York or any other city in the world?"

"It's not just that—"

"You hush. Just listen to me," Bette ordered, stopping and tapping one bare foot impatiently. "I work around men all day long, and they're not so different from us. I know, I know," she said, waving off whatever points Kelly might be inclined to make. "You dress men for a living, but you don't know what's going on behind those clothes. I do. I listen to the guys at work, day in and day out. They want someone to come home to. They want someplace to lay their heads. They want something pure and wonderful to touch their hearts. They want homes, children, mutual funds, mortgages, car payments, the whole ball of wax! I can tell you one thing for certain about Beau Sullivan." Bette shifted her weight to one long leg and looked down at Kelly with supreme confidence. "He won't come back here if there's nothing for him to come back to. So what's it going to be? Are you going to send him off with a cold shoulder or a warm kiss?"

"Whew!" Kelly shook her head and blew a shrill whistle. "You missed your calling. You should have been an evangelist! You could get those sinners up to that baptistery in no time flat." She laughed, and Bette joined in. Kelly had tears in her eyes before she brought her giggles under control. "Beau said that friends are sometimes the most important things in life, and he's right. I'm so glad you're my friend. I needed one tonight, and you came through. I owe you."

"You don't owe me a thing. I only told you what you would have figured out sooner or later."

"Maybe." Kelly looked past her to the window. "Bette, do you think I should go over to his place now and apologize for acting so stupid?"

"That's up to you." Bette let her arms dangle and shook her hands loosely at her sides. She did a couple of deep-knee bends. "I'd better be going. See you later, okay?"

"Okay." Kelly walked her to the door and stood there until Bette was out of sight, then she grabbed her purse and keys and locked up the house behind her. She went to her car, got in and drove straight to Beau's.

It was dark. The lights were on in the motor home, throwing yellow squares on the ground outside. Kelly got out of the car and walked along the side of the motor home to the door. She went over what she would say to him, how she would say it, what his responses might be. Her nerves jangled. Her head ached. Her heart raced. She wiped her palms against her skirt and took several deep breaths. She reached up to push the buzzer but froze when the door was unlatched and begun to swing out.

He'd been watching for her, waiting for her! The sly fox, she thought, pinning on a smile and getting ready to zing him with a zippy line. But then she saw the bucket, the mouth of it swooping up and out, the gray water sloshing over its rim. She had only time to release a gasp of dismay before the dirty water slapped her in the face and ran down the front of her dress.

She stood stock-still, her arms held wide, her mouth open, her eyes cast downward at the mess. Cold droplets fell from the ends of her bangs onto her face, smearing her makeup. She looked up at Beau, waiting for him to say something...do something.

"What the hell—? Oh, no. Kelly!" The empty bucket swung from his fingertips. He put his other hand to his forehead in a moment of confusion. "I didn't know you were out there! What are you doing here?"

"Dripping," she said, shaking drops of greasy water off her hands.

"Why didn't you say something, for crying out loud!"

"I didn't have time to cry out loud!"

"Well...oh, what a mess."

"May I come inside, please?"

"Yes, yes. Hell, yes!" He leaned out, gripped her elbow and helped her up the steps and inside. He set the bucket on the drainer and turned back to her. "Will that wash out? It will, of course. Take it off, and I'll wash it. I've got a mini washer and dryer, you know. Won't take a minute. Take it off."

Foot Long jumped up and down, happy to see Kelly again. Beau sent the dog a quelling glare. "Not now, Foot Long! Get in your bed. Go on. Don't give me that poor-hound-dog look."

The dachshund hung her head and dragged her long body to the wicker basket bed at the front of the motor home.

"Kelly, I'm terribly sorry about this. Your dress..."

"It's just a little dirty water," she said, looking down at herself. The seersucker material clung to her body, showing the lacy designs on her bra. "It'll dry."

"You're soaked." He stepped closer and touched her hair. The gesture sent an arrow of sentimentality through her heart. "Even your hair is wet. I'm sorry, Kelly. I didn't look. I just tossed that water out the door. I wasn't thinking."

"It's not your fault," Kelly said, laughing at his fretful tone. "Beau, you're sounding like me. Ease up, already!" She leaned sideways to stare at the bucket and mop, then she looked at the clock. "Ten-thirty and you're cleaning house?"

He placed his hands at his hips and looked down at the spotless carpet, shaking his head slowly. "Don't jump to conclusions. I'm not cleaning up because you upset me."

"What were you mopping before I came?"

"The bathroom. I was scrubbing the bathtub and the toi—" He looked at her dirty, dripping dress. "I'm so sorry, Kelly."

Then he was laughing. Then she was laughing. He reached out, grasped her shoulders and held on while he doubled over and gasped for breath, but it was a minute or two before he could speak again without breaking up.

"I bet that...that doesn't smell too good," he said between chuckles.

"Only if you don't like the smell of Shiny Bowl." She sniffed and coughed. "Personally, I think it's got a nice pine aroma, with just a dash of ammonia to give it staying power."

"It's a bit strong," he said, squinting against the sting in the air. "Are you sure you won't take it off? I'll wash it for you."

"On second thought, I think I will." She stepped around him. "It's getting kind of itchy. I guess my skin is sensitive to toilet bowl cleaner. I'll try not to mess up your clean bathroom."

"Don't worry about it. You can shower and put on that robe hanging behind the door."

"I know. I've worn it before...remember?" She glanced back at him and saw his quick wince of recall.

"I remember," he called after her. "How about a cup of coffee?"

"No, thanks. Do you have any spice tea mix left?" She closed the bathroom door and began peeling off the soaked, smelly dress.

"Sure."

"I'll take a cup of that," she called through the door as she stepped into the shower.

"Coming right up."

He had the hot tea ready for her by the time she emerged from the bathroom, wrapped in his white terry robe. Its hem dragged on the floor a good three inches. She pushed the sleeves up, but they fell down every so often to completely cover her hands. But the robe was warm and clean and smelled of Beau. She snuggled in it and sat on the couch to sip the hot tea. It was a delicious mixture of spices, oranges and cinnamon. Beau had said it was his sister's recipe.

"I'll put your dress in the washer."

"I already did," she said.

"Oh, okay." He sat in the chair.

"Sorry to interrupt your housework."

"I was just cleaning up a few things before I leave for New York," he said, staring into his teacup.

Kelly glanced at the vacuum near her feet. "And vacuuming, too, I see. Sure you're not upset?"

"Well, what if I am?" He set his cup aside so quickly that some of the tea sloshed over the rim and into the saucer. "You've got me running around and chasing my own tail! What got into you tonight?"

"Calm down," Kelly said, patting the air to placate him. "I came by here to iron some things out."

"Why are you sending me off to New York as if I'm going overseas for a year's tour of duty? Why are you pushing me away, when I know good and well that you love me and I love you?"

"Why, indeed?" Kelly said, setting her cup of tea on the table. "That's what I've been asking myself. Beau, I was confused today. I thought that you might be getting tired of me and that you wanted to travel again—alone."

"Did I say that?" He huffed out a sigh, clearly miffed at her. "I wish you wouldn't put thoughts in my head."

"I'm sorry." She went to him and sat down in his lap, taking him by surprise. "I'm a brazen woman." She kissed him, then once more. "Forgive me for being such a dope earlier? I had a case of the paranoids. We all get them from time to time, don't we?"

"I guess," he grumbled.

"Beau, I didn't mean that stuff about you treating me like a Barbie doll. One of the things I love about you is that you let me be my own person."

"I thought you might have me confused with another Sullivan," he said, still grumpy.

"Beau, do you really love me?"

"Yes, damn it! I really do!"

She smiled and kissed him again. He responded, but just barely. "And you don't want to hit the trail again?"

"Without you? No." He inched his brows together, trying to puzzle her out. "When did I ever give off those signals? I've been straight with you from the first, Kelly."

"Yes, you have. That's another reason why I love you." She looked around, pretending to be befuddled. "Why are we sitting here talking when all we really want to do is make love and make plans for many, many happy Thanksgivings and Christmases?"

He kissed her soundly, expertly. His mouth moved against hers in a full embrace as his tongue stroked and tempted. He inched back his head to look at her. "How about making some plans for anniversaries, too?"

"Yes." Her heart took wing and beat wildly in her throat. She had to swallow hard to dislodge it. When she spoke again, her voice was soft and trembling. "Many, many anniversaries. Oh, I love you so much, Beau."

He stood up with her in his arms and stepped over the vacuum cord, the mop and a plastic bag of trash as he picked his way to the bedroom.

"Beau, what about your cleaning?" Kelly asked, batting her lashes at him in an overt flutter of flirtation.

"I think I've just become a slob." He kissed her neck just under her ear, then nipped her earlobe lightly, playfully. "Make that a deliriously happy slob."

"At least I won't have to change my name," she said, smiling.

"And you've already broken in your in-laws," he noted.

"Right. You know what? Marrying you is a great idea."

"I know. That's what I've been trying to tell you during the past few weeks." He shared another smile with her.

Kelly slipped her fingers through his hair and brought his lips to hers. His kiss left no doubt of his devotion and of his firm belief in their future happiness.

As he lowered her to the bed, Kelly thanked heaven above for sending her a second Mr. Sullivan.

* * * * *

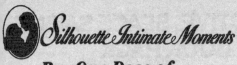

Silhouette Intimate Moments

Rx: One Dose of

```
DODD
MEMORIAL
HOSPITAL
```

In sickness and in health the employees of Dodd Memorial Hospital stick together, sharing triumphs and defeats, and sometimes their hearts as well. Revisit these special people next month in the newest book in Lucy Hamilton's Dodd Memorial Hospital Trilogy, *After Midnight*—IM #237, the time when romance begins.

Thea Stevens knew there was no room for a man in her life—she had a young daughter to care for and a demanding new job as the hospital's media coordinator. But then Luke Adams walked through the door, and everything changed. She had never met a man like him before—handsome enough to be the movie star he was, yet thoughtful, considerate and absolutely determined to get the one thing he wanted—Thea.

Finish the trilogy in July with *Heartbeats*—IM #245.

To order the first book in the Dodd Memorial Hospital Trilogy, *Under Suspicion*—IM #229 Send your name, address and zip or postal code, along with a check or money order for $2.75 for each book ordered, plus 75¢ postage and handling, payable to Silhouette Reader Service to:

In Canada	In U.S.A.
P.O. Box 609	901 Fuhrmann Blvd.
Fort Erie, Ontario	P.O. Box 1396
L2A 5X3	Buffalo, NY 14269-1396

Please specify book title with your order.

IM237-1

ATTRACTIVE, SPACE SAVING BOOK RACK

Display your most prized novels on this handsome and sturdy book rack. The hand-rubbed walnut finish will blend into your library decor with quiet elegance, providing a practical organizer for your favorite hard-or soft-covered books.

Only $9.95

Approximately 16" x 8" when assembled

Assembles in seconds!

To order, rush your name, address and zip code, along with a check or money order for $10.70* ($9.95 plus 75¢ postage and handling) payable to *Silhouette Books*.

Silhouette Books
Book Rack Offer
901 Fuhrmann Blvd.
P.O. Box 1396
Buffalo, NY 14269-1396

Offer not available in Canada.

*New York and Iowa residents add appropriate sales tax.

Silhouette Desire

COMING NEXT MONTH

#421 LOVE POTION—Jennifer Greene
Dr. Grey Treveran didn't believe in magic until he was rescued by the bewitching Jill Stanton. She taught him how to dream again, and he taught her how to love.

#422 ABOUT LAST NIGHT...—Nancy Gramm
Enterprising Kate Connors only had one obstacle in the way of her cleanup campaign—Mitch Blake. Then their heated battle gave way to passion....

#423 HONEYMOON HOTEL—Sally Goldenbaum
Sydney Hanover needed a million dollars in thirty days to save Candlewick Inn. She tried to tell herself that Brian Hennesy was foe, not friend, but her heart wouldn't listen.

#424 FIT TO BE TIED—Joan Johnston
Jennifer Smith and Matthew Benson were tied together to prove a point, but before their thirty days were up, Matthew found himself wishing their temporary ties were anything but!

#425 A PLACE IN YOUR HEART—Amanda Lee
Jordan Callahan was keeping a secret from Lisa Patterson. He wanted more than their past friendship now, but could the truth destroy his dreams?

#426 TOGETHER AGAIN—Ariel Berk
Six years before, past events had driven Keith LaMotte and Annie Jameson apart. They'd both made mistakes; now they had to forgive each other before they could be... together again.

AVAILABLE NOW:

#415 FEVER
Elizabeth Lowell

#416 FOR LOVE ALONE
Lucy Gordon

#417 UNDER COVER
Donna Carlisle

#418 NO TURNING BACK
Christine Rimmer

#419 THE SECOND MR. SULLIVAN
Elaine Camp

#420 ENAMORED
Diana Palmer

Silhouette Special Edition
NORA ROBERTS'S 50TH SILHOUETTE NOVEL

In May, SILHOUETTE SPECIAL EDITION celebrates Nora Roberts's "golden anniversary"—her 50th Silhouette novel!

The Last Honest Woman launches a three-book "family portrait" of entrancing triplet sisters. You'll fall in love with all THE O'HURLEYS!

The Last Honest Woman—May
Hardworking mother Abigail O'Hurley Rockwell finally meets a man she can trust...but she's forced to deceive him to protect her sons.

Dance to the Piper—July
Broadway hoofer Maddy O'Hurley easily lands a plum role, but it takes some fancy footwork to win the man of her dreams.

Skin Deep—September
Hollywood goddess Chantel O'Hurley remains deliberately icy...until she melts in the arms of the man she'd love to hate.

Look for THE O'HURLEYS! And join the excitement of Silhouette Special Edition!

SSE451-1